EVERY MISSING PIECE

MELANIE CONKLIN

𝔇𝔦𝔰𝔫𝔢𝔶 · HYPERION

LOS ANGELES   NEW YORK

For my father, one of the good guys

First Edition, May 2020
10 9 8 7 6 5 4 3 2 1
FAC-020093-20094
Printed in the United States

This book is set in Bell MT Pro
Designed by Phil Buchanan

Library of Congress Cataloging-in-Publication Data

Names: Conklin, Melanie, author.
Title: Every missing piece / Melanie Conklin.
Description: First edition. • Los Angeles ; New York : Disney-Hyperion,
2020. • Audience: Ages 8–12. • Summary: "Ever since her father died in a
terrible accident, Maddy Gaines has worried a lot. She calls the police
so often that she's on a first-name basis with the sheriff. When a new
boy moves to town, Maddy is convinced that he's not who he says he
is—he's a boy who went missing six months ago. Maddy, her dog, her best
friend, and her stepdad team up to see what he's hiding"—Provided by
publisher.
Identifiers: LCCN 2019044034 • ISBN 9781368048958 (hardcover) • ISBN
9781368063937 (ebook)
Subjects: CYAC: Worry—Fiction. • Stepfamilies—Fiction. • Best
friends—Fiction. • Friendship—Fiction. • Dogs—Fiction. • Family
violence—Fiction.
Classification: LCC PZ7.1.C646 Eve 2020 • DDC [Fic]—dc23
LC record available at https://lccn.loc.gov/2019044034

Reinforced binding

Visit www.DisneyBooks.com

SUSTAINABLE FORESTRY INITIATIVE

Certified Sourcing
www.sfiprogram.org
SFI-00993

Logo Applies to Text Stock Only

WHAT WAS

1

EVERYTHING GOES SOMEWHERE

The day Billy Holcomb went missing, tornadoes made me miss the bus. Technically, they were just potential tornadoes and I was hiding in the culvert when the bus blew past me, but life can go from good to bad in a heartbeat, and I'd rather be safe than sorry.

"How did he miss you?" Mom asked.

"Maybe he was in a hurry," I said.

Which was sort of true.

The middle-school bus driver has a reputation. He'll skip your stop if you aren't waiting exactly where you're supposed to be. We were three weeks into the school year, so I already knew that, but the sky had looked way too angry that morning to risk standing out in the open. Tornadoes can come from anywhere at any time.

It doesn't even have to be raining out. North Carolina may not be a tornado magnet, but there are more of them here than you might think.

"I should say something to the principal," Mom said.

Stan looked up from the little red notebook he keeps in his pocket, where he was busy writing about who-knows-what. Stan basically ceases to exist when his notebook is out. It's like his whole brain disappears inside the pages.

"Where were you standing, exactly?" he asked.

"By the bus stop."

This wasn't a lie, but it wasn't the whole truth. I *was* standing, but sort of crouched over, and not right next to the bus stop, but in the culvert next to it. The culvert is a ditch made of thick concrete, so it isn't going anywhere, even if a tornado does drop out of the sky and try to suck me up. If Mom knew the truth, she wouldn't have been mad, but she would have been *concerned.*

Those days, everyone was concerned about me. Like they all expected me to freak out because Mom and Stan got married, when really I just wished everyone would leave me alone about it.

Stan tipped his head, thinking. I swear you could see gears turning behind his eyes. If I didn't get moving, he would put the pieces together and blow my cover.

"Can you give me a ride?" I asked Mom, who sighed.

She works nights as a labor-and-delivery nurse, and she really should've been asleep by then.

"I can," Stan offered. "I need to get to the office early, anyway."

Mom smiled. "That would be great, honey. Thank you."

"But, Mom—"

"*Maddy*. I'm sure you appreciate Stan's offer." Her eyes said I did, with daggers.

Mom is always trying to get me to be cool with Stan. I don't have to pretend he's my real dad or anything, but it's still annoying how she says stuff in this pointed way, like we don't all know what's going on here. But I also know that "getting along" really matters to Mom, and that more than anything, she wants me and Stan to be friends.

"Thanks, Stan," I said.

He beamed like he'd won stepfather of the year.

It's not that I don't appreciate Stan, but he drives slower than church ladies on Sundays. Sure, there aren't any posted speed *minimums*, but there are limits to what is reasonable. Stan is from New York City, where people don't even have cars. He doesn't know how to mow the lawn or rake leaves, either. He just got his driver's license over the summer, and that was only because Mom made it a requirement for getting married, which they did in August, right before I started sixth grade. Now Mom is Sarah Wachowski instead of Sarah Gaines, but I'm still Madison—Maddy—Gaines. It's not like Stan adopted me or anything. I don't expect him to, either. When a person is right, there's a click. You fit together, like two halves of a plastic Easter egg. Stan is a good guy, but I'm pretty sure we'll never click like that.

Mom opened her arms and gave me a squeeze. "I'll miss you today."

I closed my eyes and breathed in her warm vanilla smell. Mom is taller than me, but not by much. Her side is soft and steady, and when she presses her cheek against the top of my head, I can feel her smile. She was smiling all the time those days, which I knew had a lot to do with Stan being around. Stan is tall and skinny, and he looks even taller next to Mom. She says I look like Dad, with my stick-straight hair and pointy chin, and that I'll probably grow up to be bigger than her because Dad was a tall guy, too.

Stan gathered his work computer and I followed him out to the garage, where my dog, Frankie, was asleep on her bed. She shot up the second she saw me, but I told her to sit and she plopped down, her black tail wagging. The people who say Labs are the best dogs are right.

In the car, Stan checked his mirrors and tested his brakes. He set the radio to the local station and beeped before he backed out. At the end of our court, he rolled his window down and signaled with his arm as well as his turn signal, like the dork that he is.

As we drove to school, I rested my forehead against the window and watched the familiar pattern of houses and fields roll by. Summerfield is just a stretch of highway to people passing through, but it's a nice place to live, even if we have more cows than human beings. The grocery store is a social visit and pig pickin's are regular occasions. If you need a hospital or a dry cleaner, you make the twenty-minute trip to Greensboro. The local churches hold Sunday suppers, and everyone's welcome even if you don't belong to a church, like us. The downside is that everyone knows everybody else's business, and rumors spread like wildfire.

Halfway to school, a new voice came on the radio. "—the boy was last seen crossing the street opposite his Fayetteville middle school at approximately seven forty-five yesterday morning. Foul play has not been ruled out at this time."

Goose bumps prickled along my arms.

Stan moved to switch the radio off, then hesitated.

"Authorities have issued an Amber Alert for the boy, Billy Holcomb, age eleven. He's described as a white male, approximately four and half feet tall and eighty-five pounds, with brown hair, blue eyes, and a round birthmark on his upper chest. He was last seen wearing a white T-shirt and blue jeans. Anyone with information pertaining to his whereabouts should contact their local authorities. Police say the boy may have been abducted."

This time Stan did switch off the radio, plunging us into awkward silence. For some reason, the missing boy made me think of Dad. Only my father didn't disappear.

He died.

A heavy feeling clouded my chest.

This happens sometimes when I think about Dad. It's like my body doesn't know how to live with the idea of him not being here anymore, even though he's been gone a long time. Dad died when I was eight. Now I'm eleven. But some losses keep coming back, the way a shout echoes long after it's gone. I still text him sometimes. The messages don't go through, but writing them helps. I tell him about my day, or when I'm stuck on a math problem, or when Stan really drives me bonkers. Sometimes I just say, "I love you." He never answers back.

I could feel Stan glancing at me, waiting for me to say something about the missing boy, but I kept my eyes on the road and tried my best to look like I wasn't freaking out, even though my mind was racing. What kind of kid got himself abducted right outside of his own school? Everyone knew about strangers. Don't talk to them. Don't take candy from them. And never, ever go anywhere with them. That way you don't end up plastered all over the news.

Or worse.

I swallowed hard, trying to get some moisture moving in my throat.

"Are you okay?" Stan asked. There it was again. The *concern*.

I nodded, my face going hot.

"I'm sure they'll find him," Stan said. "A large percentage of abductions turn out to be misunderstandings rather than actual kidnappings. Not that it's bad to care about things like this," he said quickly. "Your mom and I just want you to be happy." He stopped speaking then, his pale cheeks pinking up like they always did when he tried to talk to me.

It's not that I don't want to click with Stan. We're just different. Mom and I eat oatmeal. Stan likes hard-boiled eggs. We take our shoes off at the door, but Stan always forgets. We use whole milk. He drinks skim. It feels like Stan is the wrong piece for our puzzle. No matter which way I turn him, he just doesn't fit.

Stan was still watching me, so I gave him a tiny smile to show him I was okay.

9

He was right. The kid had to be somewhere.

Things can't just disappear. They can move, they can hide, they can get stuffed down inside you, but they have to go *somewhere*.

Five minutes later, we pulled into the drop-off lane at school, but when I turned to shut the car door behind me, Stan didn't give me his usual chipper wave good-bye. After a few seconds, he saw me waiting and smiled, but his smile didn't reach his eyes. He was worried again—about whether we would ever click, about whether this new family of ours would work, about whether he'd made a terrible mistake by signing up to be my stepfather. Stan liked to pretend his worries disappeared the day he married Mom, but they were right there in his eyes.

Like I said, everything goes somewhere.

2

GHOSTS

Six months later, I was going somewhere different—to a graveyard. It was the end of spring break and the daffodils were blooming, but it was still cold out. March in North Carolina is all mixed up. One day it's eighty degrees and the next it's freezing. I was more than halfway through sixth grade, but I didn't feel any older than I had at the beginning of the year. Growing up is weird like that. You feel the exact same way for ages and ages, then suddenly you look back and everything is different. You leap ahead. Growing up is like a form of teleportation, only blindfolded. You can't see where you've been until you get where you're going.

Normally, graveyards aren't my thing, but it was the last Saturday before we went back to school and I still needed a rubbing from a gravestone to finish the list of dares Cress had left for me. I'd given her a list for while she was in Trinidad, too. Whoever won had to buy the other person ice cream for two whole weeks, and I *love* ice cream. Which meant a visit to the Roach family cemetery was in order.

The Roach family cemetery is a super-secret graveyard that's hidden in the middle of my neighborhood. People say it's from the family who lived here before White Oaks became a proper subdivision with neat blacktop and streets named after trees. You wouldn't think this place held any secrets, but North Carolina is full of old stuff like that. Especially old buildings. The oldest ones are crooked and missing half their boards, like picked-over skeletons. There's no telling what you'll find in places like that, though usually the answer is ghosts.

Greensboro's most famous ghost is Lydia, the phantom hitchhiker. On rainy nights, she shows up at the side of the road and begs people for rides, but she always vanishes before they reach her destination. They say that Lydia's trying to get back home, but she never makes it there because she died on that road a long time ago.

Sometimes I wonder why Dad didn't come back as a ghost, or if maybe he did and I missed it. I don't know if I would like it if he appeared out of thin air like that, but it

would mean he was still thinking about me, even if he did scare me to death to show it.

The graveyard is on the other side of the subdivision, so I rode my bike. In our neighborhood, the blacktop is smooth and hilly, and I alternated between standing on my pedals and coasting with my feet up. When the Jessups' house came into view, I slowed down and kept my eyes peeled in case one of them was around. The Jessups' house is enormous, with a rounded section like a castle. It also happens to be located right next to the Roach family cemetery. Our house is small and looks like a triangle on top of a square, but it's big enough for the three of us, with a bedroom for me and one for Mom and Stan. Still, I can't help wondering what it's like to live in a place so big you could sleep in a different bedroom every night of the week.

A little past the Jessups' house, I stopped and stowed my bike in the ditch, where it would be less noticeable. The Jessups could be anywhere at any time, and the last time I'd seen Diesel—the biggest and rottenest Jessup of them all—he'd threatened to rip my arms off. That's the way it was between us now. We used to spend our summers swimming in the pond behind his house, but the territory wars had made us sworn enemies. Diesel started it by charging admission to his pond, and I fought back by staking out our stretch of road and nailing him with sweet-gum burs. Now Diesel says no one can use the pond without his express permission, especially *me*, which is just one example of his rottenness.

I snuck along the edge of their property until I reached the place where the woods got a little more wild, full of prickers and blackberry bushes. The Jessups kept an old double-wide back there, right up against the trees. I slipped past the trailer and slowed down, keeping an eye out for the tombstones. It always takes a minute to find them. They aren't big slabs like you see in church cemeteries. More like worn granite nubs. The first time I saw them, I thought they were monster's teeth sticking up through the leaves. Most of them don't have any writing left, but a few have dates and names for anyone brave enough to brush away the leaves.

Luckily, the ground was still clear. Once the fiddler ferns filled in, it would be impossible to find the tombstones. Here and there, baby sassafras trees offered new leaves to the sun. A sassafras tree has three types of leaves: oval, mitten shaped, and three-toed feet, which all smell like fresh oranges when you rub them between your fingers. Dad showed me that.

I spotted a gray-green tombstone poking up between

the leaves and pulled a folded piece of notebook paper from my pocket. All I needed was a quick rubbing and I'd be done with Cress's list. She was almost done with hers, but there was no way she'd steal her sister's favorite T-shirt. And if she didn't, Cress would be the one buying *me* ice cream for two whole weeks.

I grabbed a nice long stick to check for sunken spots before I knelt to scrape the gunk off the tombstone. Then I pressed the paper against the stone and rubbed my crayon over it. I was nearly finished when something moved over by the Jessups' trailer. I saw it out of the corner of my eye, in that part of your vision where you aren't sure if what you're seeing is real or not.

I jammed the paper in my pocket and hefted my stick.

My first thought was that the Night Ghost had finally decided to make an appearance. When me and Diesel were little, we made up this story about a ghost who haunts the Roach family cemetery. We called him the Night Ghost and imagined he was angry because he lost the love of his life in a high-wire accident at the county fair. That might've had more to do with our obsession with daredevils at the time, but it sure made for a scary story.

My second thought was that Diesel Jessup had come to rip my arms off. Either him or his younger brothers,

15

Devin and Donny. Devin was round as a potato, and Donny's face was always smeared with dirt. Not that there's anything wrong with a little dirt.

The Jessup boys like to act like they own this cemetery, but the land doesn't belong to them or anyone else. It's just there, hidden by the houses that surround it. Dad said it was a historic site, so it belongs to everyone. And besides, Mr. Jessup was Dad's best friend. He was there for us after Dad died, always doing stuff around the house for Mom, fixing things or moving heavy furniture. He says we're family. He would never chase me out of the cemetery.

More than anything, I wished I'd brought Frankie with me. It was a pain holding her leash while I biked, but for protection she was aces. One day last summer, we were walking in the woods when she grabbed a snake and threw it off the trail. Mom said she was probably trying to play with it, but I knew the truth: Frankie always had my back.

"Hello?" I said, wishing my voice didn't sound so small.

It was probably the Jessups. The trees were still bare except for last season's beech leaves, which hung from the branches like curled-up waffle cones. They could've spotted me through the enormous bay windows on the back of their house.

"Who's there?" I said louder. "Show yourself, coward!"

The woods remained still.

That's when I noticed something odd overhead: a hunk of wood, hanging from a rope. The rope led to the ground and disappeared into the leaves. I couldn't tell what it was tied to, but that old hunk of wood looked like it could fall out of the sky at any moment.

I took a step back.

"I wouldn't do that if I were you," a voice said from somewhere up ahead.

"That you, Diesel?"

A lanky, pale-haired boy popped out from behind the tree in front of me like a ghost appearing out of thin air. White-blond hair, skinny arms, stick-out ears.

Not a Jessup.

"Fudgesicle," I swore. "What're you doing out here?"

"I should be asking you the same thing," he replied, giving me a sly half grin. It was the kind of smile that spelled trouble, like the faded purple bruise beneath his left eye.

"I thought you were the Night Ghost."

"The who?"

"The ghost who haunts these woods. He's been pining for his long-lost love for a hundred years. He'll kill anyone who disturbs his peace."

17

The boy cocked his head. "Really? I haven't seen any ghosts out here." He probably thought I was a total weirdo who was afraid of ghosts. Which I am not.

"You know what, never mind." I took another step back. "I was just leaving anyway."

He frowned. "You'd better stop right there."

I took another step back, and my foot caught on something. By the time I looked down, that hunk of wood hanging in the trees plummeted to the ground as a rope net shot up from under the leaves and snagged my legs, leaving me dangling upside down like a squirrel in a trap.

"Told you." The boy came closer, reaching for the net.

"Stay away from me!" I shouted. "I don't need your help."

"Suit yourself."

He crossed his skinny arms and leaned back against an old oak tree while I flopped around like a fish, trying to get my sneakers free of that darn net. I finally got my legs loose, slithered to the ground, and hauled myself upright, my T-shirt and shorts all smeared with dirt.

I fixed him with a glare. "What're you booby-trapping a cemetery for anyway? That's plain silly."

He scowled. "I have my reasons."

There was something familiar about the boy's face, but I couldn't place it. For all I knew, he could be a serial killer. Plus, his baby-doll hair gave me the creeps.

"I'm leaving now," I said, slow and even. "You'd best not follow me."

His face went still as I backed away.

When I reached the edge of the little woods, I turned and ran. The boy didn't follow me, but I could feel his stare boring into my back all the way home. I rushed inside and slammed the door, but when I closed my eyes, he was all I could see.

His weird, bright hair.

His skinny arms.

That empty look on his face.

And that's when I remembered Billy Holcomb.

3

THE GIRL WHO CRIED WOLF

After Billy Holcomb went missing, he was all anyone could talk about. Missing-child flyers covered the bulletin board at the Food Lion. The Christ Baptist Church held a prayer vigil. The local news gave updates every night like they did when a hurricane was headed for town, even though he was from Fayetteville, which is clear on the other side of North Carolina.

Mom and Stan were glued to the coverage, but they always shut the TV off when I was there. When they weren't around, I watched the news reports for myself. My heart raced as I listened to Billy's father pleading for the kidnappers to let Billy come home. I studied the photo of Billy that flashed up on the screen. I imagined Billy walking to school, minding his own business—maybe staring at the ground like I always do—and someone snatching him. *Bam.* Gone. Just like that.

Now here I was, all these months later, thinking maybe I'd found him.

As I got ready to hang out with Stan for the afternoon, I went over every little detail of my encounter with the boy in the woods that morning, trying to decide what to do. You might think that as soon as I thought I'd seen a missing kid, I'd call the police.

And maybe I would have, if I hadn't already worn out my welcome.

The summer after Dad died, the electric company ran a power line through the back of our property. They mowed down the trees and blasted the bedrock. The explosives were so loud our windows shook. All I could think was that they might blow us up, too, so I called the sheriff's office to tell them about it. They said they'd look into it, which made me feel better, like maybe I'd stopped something terrible from happening. They did ask to speak to Mom, though. That was the first time I saw a ripple of concern on her face.

Later that year, I called again when our neighbors were practicing their aim on a foam deer. Their bows weren't pointed in our direction, but hearing that *thwap, thwap* noise was enough to make me break into a nervous sweat. That time, the officers weren't as friendly. We started seeing our therapist then, who made me practice deep breathing and taught me how to imagine my own private island when I wanted to call the police.

After that, I tried not to call too much, but some things needed to be seen to.

Like a lady at the mall who looked like she had a gun in her purse (it was an umbrella).

Or when the Jessups shot sparklers into people's front yards (they weren't illegal).

Or when Frankie went missing, though it turned out she was begging for treats from our neighbors, the Davises, who have a tiny bichon named Beamer (Labs are greedy like that.).

Each time I called, the deputies got a little less friendly and the worry lines on Mom's forehead got a little deeper, until they were ironed in like creases in a tablecloth. By sixth grade, Sheriff Dobbs and I were on a first-name basis. He didn't mind hearing from me every once in a while. In fact, he was so nice about my "harebrained theories" that I was pretty sure he didn't take me seriously at all. The truth is, Sheriff Dobbs and I have never seen eye to eye about what counts as an emergency. He only wants information that's "statistically sound," which means likely to be true, but I can't help it if I'm good at spotting trouble. Once you've seen the worst-case scenario, it's impossible not to see terrible prospects everywhere, like promises waiting to be fulfilled.

Then the Skate-A-Thon happened.

Every fall, our middle school holds a fund-raiser at our local roller-skating rink. I didn't go there expecting to see anything suspicious, but as Cress and I skated around the rink, I kept catching glimpses of this man who looked a lot like someone on *America's Most Wanted.* He was wearing a baseball cap with the bill pulled down, like he was trying to hide his face.

I tried not to freak out, I really did, but then I saw him taking off his skates like he was going to leave, and I had to dial 911 before he got away. Only this time when the police came, they turned off the music and locked the doors so they could check every single person to make sure the guy from *America's Most Wanted* wasn't there. Which he wasn't. It turned out the guy I saw was really someone's uncle from out of town. By the time the police finished their search, our fund-raiser was ruined and the whole school knew I'd done it.

After that, Sheriff Dobbs came over to our house to have a talk with Mom and me. He was built like a tank, with a crisp tan hat and dark brown skin. He looked at me like I was some broken, rusted thing that had been left out in the yard.

"Do you know the story about the boy who cried wolf?" he asked.

I did. It's about a shepherd boy who wanted attention, so he tricked his village into thinking wolves were attacking his flock. Everyone got tired of him lying, so when a wolf really did appear, no one answered the boy's cries for help. All his sheep got gobbled up.

"I'm sure you don't mean any harm," Sheriff Dobbs said, "but this can't happen again. If it does, there will be consequences." Mom held my hand while he used words like *false report* and *felony charges*. On the way out, he tipped his hat and said, "I'll tell you what I tell everyone, Maddy: I hope I don't see you anytime soon."

Then he gave me that look again, the one full of pity.

When your father dies unexpectedly, people don't forget. The tragedy is always there, hovering like a ghost in their words. When they look at you, they see the same person, but inside, you've changed. They can't see the change inside of you, but they can feel it. And it feels wrong to them. They wear their concern on their faces, the questions they want to ask but never will. *Do you remember him? Do you miss him?*

It's a gossiping, prying kind of concern that doesn't make you feel any better, just haunted. Even worse is how everyone thinks I freak out about everything, like emergencies aren't the kind of thing little girls should worry about, but I don't think there's such a thing as caring *too much* when it comes to saving someone's life.

All it takes is one little mistake, and your world can change forever.

For example, you can end up without a dad.

4

STAN SATURDAY

Stan was all smiles on the way into Greensboro. Mom had decided that he and I should do something fun together, just the two of us. This was our first official Stan Saturday. Maybe Mom wanted to keep me busy, or maybe she was worried about how Stan and I still weren't clicking. Either way, that's how we ended up at the ropes course in Greensboro, which is at the zoo and over forty feet tall. I'd never been there, but Stan thought it sounded fun.

The trouble with this plan was that Stan is not an outdoor guy. Like I said, he's from New York City. His idea of adventure is ordering takeout from a new restaurant. Stan works as a computer programmer. He likes things neat and orderly, not messy and unpredictable, which was why I had a really hard time imagining him swinging through the woods on the end of a rope.

When we pulled up to the course, Stan's eyes widened behind his glasses. The ropes course looks like a giant spiderweb hanging from the trees with nothing but a flimsy net to catch you if you fall.

"You really want to do that?" I asked.

"I'm sure it'll be fine," he said, more to himself than to me. "Trees are cool."

Meanwhile, all I could think about was the boy in the woods. After the Skate-A-Thon, Mom had banned me from watching *America's Most Wanted*, and Cress had made me promise never to freak out again. For six months, I'd been good. I hadn't called the police once. But seeing that strange boy made my fingers itch to call.

A strange boy who matched parts of Billy Holcomb's description. A strange boy who had no reason to be out in those woods. A strange boy who could very well be a missing kid.

I knew what I'd seen, but the tip line was for serious inquiries only, not "hysterical children." I'd been told that a dozen times. I'd be in trouble if I was wrong. So, instead of calling Sheriff Dobbs, I followed Stan toward the ropes course and certain death.

It was overcast, so there weren't many people in

line. The air had that chill we can get on spring days in North Carolina, a crisp coolness that fades as soon as the sun appears. While we waited, a nervous jiggle took up residence in Stan's foot. I could have cut him a break—after all, I was the one who'd agreed to come here—but knowing you should do something and being able to do it are two very different things.

When it comes to Stan, there's this invisible barrier between us. We're like goldfish swimming in separate bowls. What makes it even worse is that the barrier is entirely my fault. When Mom told me she thought Stan and I should spend more time together, I got upset and said some things I shouldn't have said. And Stan heard them. And now there is a barrier between us.

After a while, Stan pulled out his little red notebook and started writing. That's why he didn't notice when we reached the front of the line and the attendant asked for our tickets.

"Stan," I said.

"Hmm?" His eyes were still on his notebook. Gone.

The teenage attendant gave me a look like he wished we'd disappear, too.

"It's our *turn*," I said louder, and Stan finally snapped out of it.

He apologized, handed over our tickets, and led us to

the fitting area. While we got our harnesses, I watched the people in front of us: a mother and daughter. They were good climbers. They worked together, and when they messed up, they just laughed. They clicked.

While we waited, Stan's knee started bopping again. When they told us to go, he went the wrong way and our ropes got tangled up. Then we reached a split in the course and he turned in the opposite direction when we were supposed to be working together.

"We should go this way," I said. "See the wooden steps?"

He tilted his head, gears turning. "I don't know about that."

"Steps are better than one little rope," I snapped, followed by a quick rush of guilt.

Stan was only trying to help. He didn't even say anything back, which made it even worse. He worked his way over to me and waited while I wiped my sweaty hands and wished we'd never come to this awful ropes course in the first place.

Ahead of us, wooden steps hung from ropes like swings.

I stepped forward, and the board that had looked so stable shot out from under me, flipping me head over heels. We were in harnesses so we couldn't fall far, but I still screamed as I tipped over. For a split second, I heard the crash of the ocean and felt my father's hands on my sides, but when I opened my eyes, it was Stan who'd grabbed me. He'd fallen, too, trying to catch me. We hung there like two puppets on strings.

"Having fun yet?" he asked with a goofy smile.

My mouth fell open. "We could have *died.*"

He shook his head. "No way. You checked the harnesses five times."

"You're trusting an eleven-year-old to keep you alive," I said slowly.

"Not any eleven-year-old. A vigilant one."

I rolled my eyes. "This was a bad idea."

"Maybe. But I like 'hanging out' with you."

He did the air quotes and everything. Then he laughed at his own corny joke.

That night, I lay in bed stiff and scraped from fighting my way through the rest of the ropes course. Earlier, when Mom asked if we'd had fun, Stan had said yes, even though I'm pretty sure he hadn't had any more fun than I did. Which was pretty cool of him.

Before I go to sleep, I always check three things: First, I make sure my lamp is unplugged. Electrical appliances are major fire starters. I also make sure the path from my bed to the window is clear, in case I need to escape during the night. Most people don't know this, but you're more at risk from fire when you're asleep. We have a safety ladder below my window, just in case. Finally, I make sure that Croc is right next to me in case we need to split. As you might have guessed, Croc is a stuffed crocodile. Cress and I won him at the county fair in fourth grade. I threw the ring, but she bought the ticket, so technically he belonged to both of us. We even made up a contract to schedule sharing him, though I had custody more often those days, probably because Cress was being nice about Mom and Stan getting married and everything.

I rolled over to where Dad's picture faced me from my nightstand. He would have loved rope climbing. Dad worked as a surveyor, and in his spare time he restored the wildflower field behind our house and built a bridge across the gully, where he showed me how to catch the tiny fishes that spawned in the shallows.

My memories of Dad are like movies I can play in my mind. All it takes is a smell or a sound to trigger a memory. Only lately, the movies are playing less and less and the pictures are getting blurry. Sometimes I can't see Dad's face and I have to rush to my photo albums to remember what he looked like. It feels like I'm losing him piece by piece, and one day, he'll be gone.

"Hey," I texted him, waiting for the reply that would never come.

In the picture, Dad's smiling, his handlebar mustache tipped up at the corners. He looks like some kind of biker, but Mom says he was growing a beard for the hockey playoffs, which is when lots of hockey fans stop shaving out of superstition. I'm not in the picture with him, but the camera caught him at the perfect moment, when his eyes were looking straight into the lens.

When I stare at the picture, it feels like he's looking right at me. Like he's saying, "What is it, Maddy? What's wrong?"

I lay there for a while, telling him about Stan and rope climbing and the strange boy in the woods and how I had *not* called Sheriff Dobbs. When I finished, I felt better. I know it's just a picture and Dad can't really hear me, but it feels like he does.

5

SAFETY CHECKS

I woke up dog-tired on Sunday morning, having spent half the night searching for information about Billy Holcomb, squinting in the dark, comparing his pictures to the boy I'd met in the woods. According to the missing-person reports, Billy was four and a half feet tall and eighty-five pounds when he disappeared. The boy in the woods seemed taller than that—I'm four and a half feet now and he towered over me. That was an awful lot of growing to get done in six months, but it was possible. As far as his weight, I couldn't tell if it matched. I only weighed seventy-two pounds the last time I went to the doctor, and the boy in the woods was way skinnier than me. His face looked so similar to Billy's, but instead of a blond buzzcut, Billy had this thick mop of dark hair that covered up his ears, so I couldn't tell if they stuck out the way the strange boy's had. The hair color might not matter, though. It could've been bleached.

My heart raced so fast, looking at those photos. After everything that had happened at the Skate-A-Thon, I'd promised not to freak out again, but there I was, letting my mind run wild, making me wish I'd thought to take a picture of that boy in the woods. But I hadn't, so all I could do was go to sleep with that sinking feeling of not knowing what would happen next.

Mom's warm hand squeezed my shoulder. "You ready, Mads?"

"Yeah, sorry."

We were getting ready to do our weekly safety checks, but I was so busy thinking about Billy Holcomb that I didn't hear her at first. Once my brain gets ahold of something worrisome, it can't let go, like a dog that's got hold of a real tasty bone. In this case, I was thinking about how Billy's story had fizzled out and faded away, like he'd never gone missing in the first place. That's how it works. When something horrible happens, the newspeople care at first, but soon they move on to the next big story and forget you ever existed in the first place.

While Mom and I gathered fresh batteries, gloves, Dad's old electrical meter, and a flashlight, I wondered what that kid was doing back there in the woods anyway. Did the Jessups know him? Or was he sneaking around like me? But mostly, I wondered what he was so scared of that he built a booby trap in the middle of the cemetery.

Mom and I do safety checks once a week to make sure everything's in order in case of an emergency. We've been doing them for so long that we don't really have to think about them. They're just what we do, like vacuuming or washing dishes. We start outside, following my list:

1. Brush outside vents clean to prevent carbon monoxide buildup.
2. Trim overgrown bushes near windows and doors to eliminate hiding places for burglars.
3. Replace any dead bulbs in motion-sensor lights.
4. Make sure the water heater is set no higher than 120 degrees to prevent burns.
5. Test all smoke alarms and replace batteries as needed. Clean the grilles.
6. Test the rescue ladder under my bedroom window.
7. Check the fire extinguisher under the kitchen sink.

8. Test the emergency call button and change
batteries if needed.

We ordered the emergency call button from a commercial. It's the kind for older people who've fallen and can't get up. I had to promise never to press it without Mom's permission. (Unless Mom is ever unconscious. Then I get to make the call.)

I brushed the dryer vent while Mom trimmed the bushes. I wanted to ask her about Billy Holcomb. If she knew I was worrying about some kid who went missing six months ago, she'd flip, but maybe there were other questions I could ask.

"Hey, Mom. Do you know if anyone new moved into the neighborhood?"

"Not that I know of," she said, her mouth in a frown as she concentrated on the bushes.

"What about the Jessups? Do they have family in town?"

"I don't think so. Why?"

"No reason," I said, moving on to the next task.

My grandparents don't think safety checks are the best thing for me, but Mom is okay with them. She knows I like to be prepared. We talk about how none of these emergencies are likely to happen, and how it's okay to spend a little bit of time thinking about them, but not too much. I try not to overdo it, but it's hard to know how much is too much. If you spend a year hiding in a culvert at the bus stop, and one day out of 365 days there is a tornado, people would say you were smart and prepared. But if the tornado doesn't come, you're overreacting.

It's a fine line.

It's not like I have some kind of superpower that can protect me from terrible things, but once you look at a situation and ask yourself what could go wrong, you see the world differently. Mom says I'm brave, but the therapist we see calls it anxiety, which is a normal reaction to stressful situations. The goal is to have balance.

While we did our safety checks, I thought about Billy and almost asked Mom for an emergency call button to put at the bus stop in case anyone tried to abduct *me*, but I was pretty sure she wouldn't like that idea. Besides, one of the Jessups would probably push it and get me into even more trouble. That would be just like Devin or Donny.

In the end, I decided it was smarter not to ask.

Some things are better left unsaid.

6

KISS MY GRITS

Sometimes I think I must be seeing things, like when I climbed onto the bus after spring break and saw the boy from the Roach family cemetery sitting in my seat. His white-blond head stuck up from the back row, which is where I sit every single day unless Diesel Jessup decides to be a jerk and forces me out. Cress was back there, too, but I dropped into one of the open seats in the middle of the bus before the boy from the cemetery could spot me.

The bus rattled on as my mind flooded with questions. Why was he riding our bus? Did he live here now? And was his hair actually bleached, or was I imagining it?

At the next stop, Cress slid into my seat and I threw my arms around her.

"Hey, watch the hair!" She pulled back and smoothed a hand over the side of her head, pausing to fix one of the pins holding her tight black curls into a neat ponytail.

"Why are you sitting up here?" she asked. "Are you mad at me or something?"

"No, it's just—" How was I supposed to start? How do you tell your best friend that the kid in the back of the bus might be a boy who went missing six months ago without sounding weird? Maybe the police had gotten it wrong, and Billy was still in trouble. Otherwise, how would he end up all the way in Summerfield, looking like he was hiding who he was? This kid could be Billy Holcomb, and he could need my help. Not that anyone would ever believe me . . .

"Earth to Mads," Cress said, making me jump.

"Sorry."

"What's up?"

I hesitated, and she frowned. "Don't make me use the blood oath."

We'd taken advantage of an unfortunate bike accident over the summer to write our initials in blood on this big rock at the front of my driveway. The blotchy letters had faded, but as long as we told each other the truth, we were good. We had a blood oath.

"Do you see that boy back there?" I said, feeling awkward.

She turned to look and I tugged her back down. "Don't! He'll see you."

"Who?" Cress asked, squinching her dark eyes at me. Cress believes in science and math and things that can be measured or tallied. She was not going to like my story.

"That boy in the back. The one with the baby-doll hair and the stick-out ears."

"The new kid? His name is Eric."

Her words sunk in. It wasn't him. It wasn't Billy.

The ball of nervous energy that had gathered in my stomach loosened a bit.

"Do you know him or something?" Cress asked.

By *him* she meant Eric. Eric who was *not* Billy.

I sighed, letting my head flop against the vinyl seat. "I ran into him in the woods behind the Jessups' house. He was back there by the trailer."

"He got on the bus with Diesel," Cress said.

I scrunched my nose and Cress laughed. She had no reason to like Diesel, either. Not since he tried to kiss her cheek during recess last year. I'd flung a rock at him, hitting him square in the eye. He'd ended up with an eye patch, and I'd ended up in trouble.

"Come on, Diesel's not that bad," she said. "He started helping out at the science center on the weekends, you know. He's a goat herder."

"Diesel at the science center? No way."

She rolled her eyes. "Did you notice what I'm wearing?" She turned so I could see the front of her T-shirt, which said *Kiss My Grits.*

"Holy carrots! Mia's gonna kill you!"

"I asked to borrow it, but she said no. She has no idea I took it from the laundry basket."

"Serves her right. She's always taking our freezer pops."

"And saying she didn't," Cress added.

"And calling us babies," I said, thinking about how Mia made fun of us for not wearing makeup the last time I slept over at Cress's. I'd told Mia she could look like a clown if she wanted but I was perfectly fine how I was, thank you very much.

Cress did a little dance in her seat. "Looks like I beat you. Sorry, not sorry!"

"Oh yeah?" I pulled the rubbing from my bag and unfolded it over our laps.

She traced a finger over the date: January 12, 1859. "Wow. That's super old."

"I know, right? It's creepy to think there are bodies out there in the woods."

"There might not be. The corpses would have decomposed by now, even if they were buried in coffins. The human body is made of seventy percent water. Once all that water evaporates, there's nothing left but bones and big pockets of air."

I thanked heavens Dad had been cremated. "So I guess we tied?"

Cress bit her lip, thinking. "Listen. I'll buy your ice cream and you buy mine. Deal?"

I laughed and she did a goofy silent cheer, shaking her shoulders back and forth like she was doing the limbo. I pulled Croc from my bookbag. "Here, it's your turn."

She looked at Croc, then me. "Why don't you keep him until you come over on Friday?"

I buried my face in Croc's fuzzy neck. Secretly, I was glad I didn't have to let him go.

I kept my head down on our way into school, both to dodge the rain and to avoid Eric. I felt silly for freaking out about him when he was only some random new kid. But then I reminded myself of all the things that didn't add up: how much he looked like Billy Holcomb, his fake hair, and the fact that he got on the bus with Diesel Jessup. Was he staying with the Jessups or what?

While Cress went to her locker, I went to the library in search of answers. The library is my favorite place. I swear you can feel the knowledge entering your body through your nose.

When I was little, Mom and I went to the Benjamin Branch library downtown. That's where Mom and Stan met. Mom was returning a giant stack of books, so she was pushing the door with her elbow when it suddenly popped open and the books fell out of her arms—right onto Stan's foot. Stan had recently moved to town for a new job. He was getting his library card, and he says meeting Mom there is one more example of how awesome libraries are.

"Morning, Miss Rivera," I called to the dark-haired lady standing over by a book display that read, *March Madness: Sixteen books enter, but only one book wins!*

"Good morning, Maddy." She turned, and I read the front of her T-shirt, which featured a green Minecraft zombie and the phrase *Devour Books, Not Brains.* A pair of gold book earrings hung from her ears. She shifted so I could see the display better. "Have you voted this week?" she asked. "We'll have our March Madness winner soon."

I'd read all of the books, but my favorites were the one about the island girl who was searching for her long-lost mother and the one about the boy trapped in the well.

"I liked *Hurricane Child* and *Hello, Universe.*"

"Excellent selections. Make sure to officially cast your votes." She handed me two red slips of paper, and I signed them and dropped them in the voting jars.

"Hey, Miss Rivera . . . do you know if we got a new student today?"

"Yes, I believe we did."

"Is his name Eric?"

"Yes. Eric Smith." She gave me a curious glance.

"Thanks. See you tomorrow." I turned around, feeling a little better. At least now I could search the kid's name.

Then I saw Diesel Jessup standing by the library doors.

I pushed past him, but he followed me into the hall.

"I heard you were on our property again," he said, looming over my shoulder.

"From who?" I didn't care if this Eric kid ratted me out. Diesel would still have to wring a confession out of me.

His nostrils flared like they did when he was fibbing. "No one."

"If no one saw me, then I guess I wasn't there."

"Yes, you were."

"I was not. I was in the graveyard."

"Same difference."

"No, it isn't!" I yelled. The kids in the hall froze. "There's this thing called a property line. I didn't cross yours. Why're you so worried about me going back there, anyway?"

"I'm not." Another lie.

Diesel leaned closer, his huge head blocking out the light. "Listen, Gaines. You stay off our property and leave Eric alone," he whispered in his nastiest voice. "You may think you know better, but you don't. For once in your life, don't be a freak."

Now, we'd said some terrible things in our territory wars, but this was a new level of terrible, even from Diesel. I could feel my face turning red as a tomato while everybody around us stared. I hate how some people do that, poking at the softest part of a person to make them hurt. And I hate that it always works on me.

Diesel turned to walk away.

"Kiss my grits," I said, half under my breath.

He stopped. "What did you say?"

"I said: Kiss. My. *Grits!*"

A few kids snickered, and for a split second Diesel looked less than sure of himself. Then he puffed his chest and said, "That doesn't even mean anything!"

He stomped off as kids jeered and booed because they didn't get the fight they wanted. I turned around and went the other way, even though it would make me late for math. I didn't care what Diesel Jessup said. If he wanted a war, I'd give him one.

7

WELCOME WAGON

I searched Eric's name five ways from Sunday and didn't once find a picture that matched him. Which made no sense. As people live their lives, they leave trails. School pictures. Soccer teams. Blue ribbons for pie-eating contests. Whatever it is, every person leaves their mark.

Except for Eric Smith.

His trail was a total dead end.

For the next two days, I thought about what to do while the sky wrung itself out. All day long, rain drizzled like a leaky faucet. At night, thunder shook the house. With all that water coming down, the creek behind our house swelled so high we could see it from our windows.

Angry water boiled over the lip of the gully like a fountain, right where Frankie liked to swim.

All that time, I kept thinking about how Diesel had bossed me, and how much I wanted to prove him wrong. I didn't care what he said. I'd go where I pleased when I pleased—but maybe not in the rain. Nothing feels grosser than cold, dirty water spraying up your backside as you bike.

By the time I got home from school on Wednesday, the Carolina blue was showing in the sky again, but instead of heading out, I hovered in the kitchen while Mom baked, wanting to go to the cemetery and investigate but dreading what might happen if I did.

When Mom bakes, she hums. Especially when she's making pies. She mixes the dough and rolls it out with a pin made of solid red cedar. Dad carved it for her when they first got married. Her hands move quickly, and when she lifts the crust it's in one smooth swoop, like a bird taking flight. She crimps the edge and fills the pie with any number of delicious ingredients: pumpkin custard, strawberry rhubarb, caramel, pecans, chocolate mousse. This time it was chocolate chips and walnuts for a Toll House pie, which tastes as good as it sounds.

Once the pie was in the oven, Mom wiped her hands

on the old, flowered apron from Grandma Evans and fixed an eye on me. "What's on your mind, Mads?"

"Nothing," I said, pretending the dish towel on the counter was super interesting. Really, it was super fatal—or at least it should've been for the blue bottle fly buzzing around the room. I snapped the towel at the fly and missed. Darn things are impossible to catch.

Mom made a face: huge eyes with her eyebrows sky-high. Soon she'd come after me, pecking me with kisses and saying "What's eating you?" over and over until I cracked.

"Fine." After what happened last fall at the Skate-A-Thon, I'd promised Mom I wouldn't do this again. But here I went. "There's this kid down at the Jessups'."

"What kid?"

"He showed up last week. I think he's staying there. He started going to our school, and Diesel warned me to stay away from him. Don't you think that's weird?"

"Maybe they're helping someone out."

"But why would Diesel tell me to stay away?"

"Hmm." Mom finished cleaning off the cutting board and dropped her measuring cups into the sink. "They might want some privacy. I wouldn't worry about it."

"I'm not worrying."

Mom gave me her concerned face, which is why

I hadn't wanted to talk to her about any of this in the first place. "Remember," she said, "not everything is an emergency."

"I *know*. I just don't like Diesel Jessup telling me what's what." I whipped the dish towel at the fly again and nailed him. Frankie rushed over to gobble up the evidence.

Mom gave me a funny look, then smiled. "You know what might be nice? A welcome wagon. I have a pie box from the bakery, and there's nothing like a fresh Toll House pie."

"*I* want a fresh Toll House pie."

"Then maybe you can share some with your new friend," she said.

My mom is smooth like that.

It's not easy biking with a pie box on your handlebars and a dog on a leash, but somehow me and Frankie and the pie made it to the Jessups' in one piece. As we walked into the woods, I kept my eyes peeled for anything weird hanging from the trees. Unfortunately, looking up like that meant I didn't spot the twine strung *between* some trees until my foot was about to hit it.

I twisted fast, juggling the pie box and Frankie's

leash and almost falling. Maybe this wasn't such a good idea after all. If Diesel saw me, he was gonna kill me.

Frankie pulled at her leash and whined. Her amber eyes were sure and steady.

"You're right," I said. "Diesel Jessup can't keep me from walking around my own neighborhood." I gathered the pie box and Frankie's leash and stepped around that booby trap like I had every right to be there. We were the welcome wagon, after all.

I scanned the woods, wondering where to look for Eric. Back here? Or up at the house? I stopped to look around, but Frankie kept pulling me toward the old trailer, her tail wagging. We slipped around the side and found the door hanging open. Frankie yipped, and wouldn't you know it, Eric popped his head outside like he'd been waiting for us.

"What are you doing here?" he asked.

I tried not to drop the pie while Frankie tugged on her leash, struggling to get to him.

He stepped down to the ground. "It's okay. I like dogs."

I let her go, and she covered his face in kisses like the traitor that she was.

When she finished, Eric looked at me. "What do you want?" he asked. The bruise beneath his eye had faded to a rotten yellow-green. Meanwhile, my mind was racing with all the questions I had, about where he came from, why he was here, who he *was*.

I plastered a huge smile on my face and lifted the box. "My mom sent a Toll House pie."

"For real?"

"Yeah. We're the welcome wagon."

He took the box and cracked it open, taking a deep whiff. He started to smile, then shook his head. "You shouldn't be here."

"Are you staying here or something?"

"Yeah. For now."

He stared at the ground, scuffing his sneaker toe in the leaves, and I stood there wondering why he was out there in that trailer. If he was visiting the Jessups, wouldn't he stay in their huge house? He had short hair, but if it was longer, bushy on the sides, and as dark as his eyebrows . . . he'd look a lot like Billy Holcomb. I got that goofy feeling in my guts like I was about to tip over the edge of something. It was the same feeling I got when I waited for a tornado at the bus stop: the creeping certainty that something terrible was about to happen.

"I'm Maddy," I said. "I live in the neighborhood. Your name is Eric, right?"

I was waiting for him to say it. *No, my name is Billy Holcomb.*

"Yeah," he said. "With a *C*."

There was that bad feeling again, reminding me that I was full of nonsense.

Behind him, the trailer door banged open and a skinny white lady with black hair and ratty jean shorts appeared. Her eyes narrowed when she saw me. "Who in blazes is this?"

"Someone from school," Eric said.

She frowned. "Did you forget what we said about having people over?"

"She brought us a *pie*," he said, lifting the box.

"Oh." She gave me a tight nod. "Thank you, then."

"I'm Maddy Gaines. Nice to meet you."

Instead of introducing herself, she glared at me something fierce and reached for Eric.

He jerked away.

"We talked about this," she said in a low voice. When Eric didn't answer, she sighed. "Jessamyn's making her famous dumplings tonight. You should come help."

Eric shook his head, his eyes fixed on the ground.

"Look, I'm sorry I got stuck at work today."

He shrugged. "Whatever."

She fixed me with another glare. "Say good-bye to your friend and come on up to the house." Then she headed into the Jessups' yard without saying another word to me.

Meanwhile, Eric stood there not talking, which made this awful buzz build up in my stomach.

"I guess I'll see you later," I said, pulling Frankie back the way we'd come.

After a minute, Eric jogged to catch up with us. He patted Frankie while he led us around his booby traps, not saying a darn thing. Of course I couldn't think of anything to say, either—until I got to my bike and found the Jessup brothers standing on top of it.

"Hey! Leave that alone!"

Diesel lifted his foot to smash my tire. "I warned you not to trespass."

"I was just dropping off a pie. Let's call a truce, okay?"

"And if I don't? What're you gonna do, sic your dog on me?" He made a face at Frankie and she had the good sense to growl back at him.

"Let her go," Eric said.

Diesel pointed at Eric. "You shouldn't be talking to her, anyway."

Eric scowled but didn't argue.

"Please," I said, even though begging Diesel made me want to barf. I loved that bike. Dad and I spent ages cleaning it up. We even repainted the body, which used to be pale pink but is now midnight blue. It had gotten too small for me, but I couldn't give it up.

Diesel stared at me for a second, then gave my tire a kick and walked off. Devin, the round middle brother, made a rude gesture, and the dirty-faced little one, Donny, spat on the seat. He wasn't even old enough to tie his shoes, but he already knew the Jessup ways.

As soon as they left, I hopped on my bike and pedaled away with Frankie running next to me. I was halfway down the road before I realized I hadn't said good-bye to Eric, but when I glanced back over my shoulder, he was already gone.

8

UNKNOWN QUANTITIES

"What do you think of paddle boats?" Stan asked on Saturday, a few days after my visit to Eric's place. I was wiped out from staying over at Cress's. As usual, we'd barely slept. We were too busy talking about Mia's new boyfriend, who had texted her at dinner and gotten her phone taken away.

"I don't think of paddle boats at all," I joked, swallowing a yawn.

Mom made a face.

"But sure." I stabbed at the peas in my shepherd's pie. "Paddle boating sounds fun."

Which it could be. They had these new swan boats at the science center. I'd seen them bobbing around on the water like giant bath toys.

Stan looked up from consulting the newspaper. "Oops. Looks like the paddle boats aren't open until April, but we could go to the observatory. They have a meteor show on Saturday."

"They do?" That actually did sound fun.

"The Gamma Normids should be active this week. They're the biggest show during March," he said, which made me laugh. His pale cheeks pinked up. "What?"

"Sorry. That sounds goofy, you know. 'Gamma Normids.' What's next, the Beta Abnormids?" I cracked up, and wouldn't you know it, Stan actually let out a laugh. He was usually so serious, writing in his notebook all the time.

Mom was smiling so hard at the two of us that I had to take it down a notch. I didn't want her expectations to get out of whack or anything.

"I'm going to put my feet up for a bit," she said. "Anybody need anything before I go?"

"I've got it," Stan said, hurrying to take her plate and cup before she could clear it.

"Thanks, hon." She pecked him on the cheek and I looked away fast.

It didn't make me mad, seeing them together like that, but it didn't feel right, either. Like I was betraying Dad somehow, merely by watching it happen.

Once Mom was gone, Stan came back to the table and spread his paper between us. "Want to help me with the jumble?" The word jumble is usually my favorite. I love looking at those scrambled-up letters and waiting for my brain to sort them into the right order.

But there was that darn barrier again.

"No thanks," I said, pretending not to see the hurt on Stan's face. I should've been able to sit there with him. It shouldn't have been a big deal. But suddenly all I wanted was to go to my room and lie next to Dad's picture so I could talk to him. It's funny how missing Dad always seems to follow talking to Stan, like Stan is haunted by Dad's ghost. Only Stan doesn't know it.

The observatory is a small white building with a weird metal dome that opens up to the stars like a sunroof, only I guess it's more of a moonroof because it's mainly open at night. I'd never been there before, but Stan told me all about it on our drive over. They had telescopes for viewing astronomical objects like the Gamma Normids meteor shower, which was winding down but should still have been fun to look at.

"Going to the observatory," I texted Dad as Stan and I walked across the parking lot. It felt a little strange telling him about our Stan Saturdays, but Dad would have loved the idea of looking at the stars. Maybe he wouldn't mind that I was going with Stan.

"How's everything at school?" Stan asked out of the blue.

"Pretty good." I repositioned the gum in my mouth. I was trying to blow one last bubble before I threw it out.

"Your mom said you met a new boy in the neighborhood?"

I about choked on my gum. "Yeah. Eric."

"Is he nice?"

I thought about Eric petting Frankie. "Yeah, he's nice. Kind of weird, but nice. Like you," I said, and immediately regretted it. I swear it's like my mouth has a mind of its own sometimes.

The barrier started to slide into place, but Stan just smiled. "You're right. I am weird. I was a weird kid, too. I didn't have many friends. I preferred collecting rocks."

I laughed, and he said, "No, seriously. Rocks are much better friends than most kids."

"You made friends with rocks?"

"I did. There's no shame in that, as long as you don't expect the rocks to talk back. The truth is, we're all weird. Every human being is an unknown quantity."

Stan called strangers *unknown quantities*. Like his new

boss at work. He couldn't say if he liked her yet. He'd have to get to know her first. I felt the same way about new teachers. It took at least a month until I knew if I liked them. That first week of school could be awesome, but it might not last. There were exceptions, though. I knew Miss Rivera was awesome the minute I met her. And then there were people like Diesel, who only got worse over time.

"Some people are jerks, though."

"I don't know about that," Stan said. "People are complicated. The ones who don't have many friends are usually the ones who need them the most."

That idea caught in my mind. I was pretty sure Diesel was a lost cause, but maybe Eric just needed a friend. He was probably in the woods right then, rigging up more booby traps.

I paused at the doors to the observatory, taking in the curved metal ceiling, which looked taller from the inside. My gum went in the trash, and Stan and I went to find an open telescope. We started with the moon. Then Mars and Venus. By the end we watched for meteors burning up as they entered Earth's atmosphere. Without the telescope, those streaks looked white, but up close they were a mix of every color. Plus, the sky was chock-full of stars. I mean every single inch. I've lain on our roof plenty of nights, but I'd never seen anything like this.

"Amazing, isn't it?" Stan said.

"Yeah. I never knew all of that was up there."

"Exactly. What we know to be true depends entirely on our point of view."

I looked at him watching the sky through his glasses, and for a few moments, the barrier lifted. Not enough to go away forever, but enough to stand there together, staring at the stars.

9

BAIT & TRAP

Diesel may have done his best to scare me off, but there was no way he was keeping me from talking to Eric again. I could smell their secrets the way Frankie smells a squirrel. She can't always see them, but she knows they're there, and she doesn't give up until she finds them.

On Sunday morning, after safety checks and a breakfast of pork sausage and eggs, I clipped Frankie's leash and told Mom I was going to fetch her pie plate, even though it was one of those cheap aluminum pans that people usually toss in the recycling bin.

"Have fun with your new friend," she called as we went out the door, which made me frown. She had that tone in her voice like she knew what was up, but I wasn't sweet on Eric.

"Wish me luck," I texted Dad.

The closer I got to the Jessups', the more my heart thumped. I told myself to relax, but as their house came into view, the blood rushing in my ears turned to the *crash, crash, crash* of the waves. Instead of leaving my bike in the ditch by the road, I pushed it behind the neighbor's holly bushes and ran for the woods with Frankie galloping beside me, her ears flapping.

When we got to the tree line, I pulled up short and scanned for enemies. The woods seemed quiet, like maybe no one was home. I pulled Frankie closer to the trailer, keeping an eye out for Eric's booby traps. She gave a little whine.

"Hush," I said. "We don't want to get caught poking around, now, do we?"

Frankie beamed up at me, her tail whipping.

I climbed a stump next to the trailer to look inside, but the blinds were drawn. My heart raced as I peeked around every edge. I could only see slivers of curtains, a bed, a mirror. Nothing useful, which made me feel kind of bad for spying. Not to mention what Mom would think if she found out. This was exactly the kind of thing she didn't want me doing. But what if I was right? What if Eric really was Billy Holcomb and he needed my help?

Before I could figure out what to do next, Frankie

made her happy whine and Eric's pale head popped around the corner of the trailer.

I scrambled down from the stump. "Hey! I was just looking for you."

He frowned. "Diesel's gonna flip if he finds you here."

"He's jealous I'm winning the war is all."

"What war?"

"It's a ridiculous territory war, but I won the entrance to the subdivision in the sweet-gum battle, so he's mad. I can't use the pond, but he can't leave the neighborhood."

Eric laughed and his whole face went from stormy to bright. "Diesel says you're always in everybody else's business. Did you really call the cops on him last summer?"

My face went hot. I *had* called the police, but Diesel and his brothers had been shooting sparklers into people's yards. They could've burned someone's house down.

"I don't care what Diesel says," I said, giving the stump a good kick. "He's a jerk."

Eric stopped laughing, and I scolded myself for talking mess about Diesel in front of him. If they were friends, that sure as heck wasn't going to get me inside that trailer.

Meanwhile, Frankie was giving herself a conniption trying to reach Eric, so I let her go and she jumped on him, licking all over his face and his stick-out ears. I don't know what it is about ears, but Frankie loves them.

He rubbed her head and smiled. "I wish I had a dog."

"You should get one."

"My dad says dogs are good for two things: eating up all your food and giving you fleas."

"Frankie doesn't have fleas! I give her special treats to keep the bugs off."

At the sound of her name, Frankie beamed at me, her long pink tongue lolling out of the side of her mouth like a yo-yo.

"She's a girl?" Eric asked.

"Yep." We got Frankie the year Dad died. Mom didn't know Frankie was a girl when we named her, and by the time we figured it out, I decided a girl could have any name she wanted.

"I need to get our pie plate back," I said. "Do you have it?"

"I think so." He stood up and looked at the saggy old trailer like he wasn't sure about taking me in there, but then he made up his mind and led us over.

The key to catching a squirrel is using a trap, which sounds harsh but isn't. Dad and I had to use one once, for a young mama squirrel who'd built a nest in our garage. Dad would've let the squirrel stay, but it was too hot in the rafters for her babies to survive. We used peanut butter as bait, and soon she was back in the woods where she and her babies belonged.

I'd baited my trap with the world's best pie.

Now it was time to see what I'd caught.

I stopped to tie Frankie up, but Eric said, "It's okay," and held the door for both of us.

My stomach swirled as I stepped inside.

I'd expected it to be all dark and moldy in there, but someone had given the linoleum a good scrub, and the air smelled like fresh paint and pine cleaner. The couch looked new, too. Cute mismatched chairs circled the kitchen table, and a hand-painted sign hung over the sink: *Life Is a Work in Progress.* Other than some trash piled by the door, it was nice. The only weird things were these broken bowls lined up along the kitchen counters. The cracks were shiny, like they'd been filled with metal or something. Which was odd, but not any kind of clue.

"Why are all these bowls broken?" I asked, picking one up. It was cold to the touch and surprisingly heavy.

"Kelsey makes them," Eric said.

Kelsey. So that was the name of the woman I'd seen here before.

"Is she your mom?"

He gave me a stony look, so I tried again. "Does she sell these or something?"

"Sometimes." He went into the kitchen and opened the oven door. The inside was chock-full of pots and pans, including our pie plate. "We don't bake much," he said as he handed me the plate, which made me feel pretty terrible for wishing I'd kept the whole pie for myself.

"Is Kelsey here?"

He gave me a funny look. "No, she's at work."

I breathed a sigh of relief, knowing she wouldn't barge in. I could do without her glare searing into my skin. "What does she do?"

"She's been helping Diesel's dad at the construction office, doing paperwork and stuff."

That made sense. Mr. Jessup was a contractor, which was part of the reason why they had such a big, fancy house. My mind raced, thinking of other questions to ask.

"Where'd y'all move from?"

He looked down, stubbing his toe. "Asheville."

Which is clear on the other side of the state from Fayetteville, where Billy went missing.

A sinking feeling gathered in the pit of my stomach. I'd hoped there would be some kind of clue inside this trailer, but I didn't see anything that tied Eric to Billy Holcomb. There were other questions I could ask, but you can only pry so much before a person gets ornery.

"Want a Cheerwine?" Eric asked.

I gave him a thumbs-up. Cheerwine is only the best soda in the whole wide world. While he poured red soda into plastic cups, I looked in the Winnie-the-Pooh jars on the counter. The first one held flour. The second, sugar. And the third held a thick wad of cash.

There is nothing like a pile of money to make your heart skip a beat. I set the lid down as fast as I could without breaking it.

Eric handed me my cup. "I'm sorry about your daddy," he said, his voice soft but serious. "Diesel said he was a hero. That he saved your life."

For a split second, I felt naked as a freshly shucked corncob. "Diesel said that?"

"Yeah."

"Well, that's none of his business. Or yours."

"I'm not saying that to be mean. Anyway, I'm sorry he's dead, but at least he was good."

I didn't know what to say to that. You don't thank someone for reminding you that your father is dead. But you aren't supposed to yell at them, either.

"What about *your* dad?" I asked.

Eric frowned like he was about to say "none of your business," and I felt bad for prying so hard, but then Frankie came over and started licking his chewed-up fingers, probably tasting all the spit he'd left there. Dogs can be gross like that.

Eric rubbed her ears and she head-butted him. He laughed, and suddenly he didn't look so mysterious anymore, even though he had a cookie jar full of money and those dark eyebrows that didn't match his Barbie doll hair and that face like Billy Holcomb's.

He looked like a kid who could use a friend.

The truth is, you can bait your trap with peanut butter, but that doesn't mean you'll always get squirrels. Sometimes you'll catch a possum.

That's what happened the first time Dad and I tried to catch that mama squirrel in the garage. We filled the squirrel trap with bait, but what we found the next day was a possum lying in it, all limp and not moving. Dad was upset at first because he thought the possum was dead. He got a broom to push it out of the garage, but as soon as he touched it, the possum rolled over and hissed at us with these giant yellow teeth. We both screamed bloody murder.

"I better go," I said, and Eric walked out to the road with me and Frankie. That time, before I rode away, I turned back and waved good-bye.

10

THE LIVING MUSEUM

*E*ric didn't show up for school the following Thursday. I sat in the library wondering where he was while Miss Rivera told us that we were going to spend the next few weeks building a Living Museum. That didn't sound too exciting at first, but then she explained that we were going to dress up like historical figures and tell their stories, which was kind of cool.

"Countless people have made important contributions to our world," Miss Rivera said. She was dressed as Amelia Earhart, though her goggles looked more like the science kind than the airplane kind. "Each of you will identify a historical figure, research their contribution to the world, and share their story in our Living Museum. Remember, stories are the language of history. We share stories of the past to prepare for the future. Plus, it's fun to dress up."

She struck a pose, and everyone laughed.

Next to me, Cress was already circling names on the list of historical figures we'd been given. She'd also written another list of her own ideas. Miss Rivera said that if we had a figure in mind who wasn't on the list, we could make our case for them to get approval. The best costumes and speeches would win prizes. First place was a gift card to the Dollar Tree and a special pizza lunch with Miss Rivera, which wasn't half bad.

"You will begin your research this morning in the library," Miss Rivera said. "This project is across departments, so you'll also get the opportunity to create props during Art and write your speech and long-form essay in English Language Arts. You're welcome to work here during lunch or study hall at the end of the day—the choice is yours. Remember, as Amelia Earhart said, 'The most effective way to do it is to *do it.*' Now break!"

Nervous chatter broke out as everyone started talking about who they might become.

Cress chewed her lip. "I can't decide who I want to be."

"You don't have to choose right now."

"I don't want to waste any time. You'll help me with the props, right? You're so good at making models. I hate papier-mâché. It feels like cold snot."

I laughed. "Sure, I'll touch the snot for you."

She smiled in relief. "Thanks."

I followed her over to the computers, thumbing my list. Cress's mom is a big-time attorney whose favorite saying is "Don't put off till tomorrow what you can do today." Sometimes I think Cress takes that too seriously. I liked doing a good job in school, but I wasn't the best in my class. And I had absolutely no idea who I wanted to be. It felt like a big responsibility, bringing history to life. An idea caught in the corner of my mind, but it scuttled away before I could grab hold of it, like a crawfish jetting under a rock.

While Cress hemmed and hawed over whether she should be Michelle Obama or Katherine Johnson, I typed in "Hillary Clinton" and started reading, but I couldn't concentrate.

My mind kept wandering back to Eric.

It would be so easy to make friends and act like everything was normal. Then I wouldn't have to worry about disappointing Mom or getting in trouble with Sheriff Dobbs. But then I thought of Dad, and how I could barely remember the feel of his hand in mine. How he was here one day and gone the next, and I knew I couldn't act like everything was normal.

Because it wasn't.

There was something weird going on with that kid.

Cress was busy making a list of pros and cons, so I brought up Billy Holcomb's picture again to see if I'd missed anything. Some small scar or mole that was an undeniable match to Eric. This one picture came up over and over again: an old school photo where Billy isn't really smiling, just sort of staring at the camera. He's squeezed into a faded T-shirt that's way too small for him, and his hair is so big and bushy that it puffs out like a helmet.

Eric's and Billy's faces were so similar, but Eric's cheeks were leaner and Billy's skin was more tan. Eric was pasty white, like he hadn't been outside much lately. Plus, Billy's hair was brown, and I couldn't see any stick-out ears hiding under it, but they did have the same dark eyebrows and half smile. The longer I looked, the faster my heart raced.

"What's that?" Cress asked.

I shut the window. "Nothing. I was checking something." After the Skate-A-Thon, I'd promised Cress that I'd stop freaking out. She didn't want me to be the school weirdo, either.

Her eyes squinched up. "That was the kid who went missing last fall, wasn't it?"

"Maybe."

"Why're you looking at pictures of him?"

I winced. Could I really tell her what I thought about Eric without her thinking I was freaking out again? "Well . . ."

She rolled her eyes. "Blood oath, remember?"

I took a deep breath. "You know that kid Eric?"

"Yeah?"

"I think . . . I think he might be that kid who went missing last fall."

As soon as I said it, I felt silly as a goose.

Cress brought Billy's picture back up on the screen and studied it. She stared and stared at his face while she worried at her lip like she was going to chew it clean off.

"You know what," she said. "I think you might be right."

11

PATTERNS

A ccording to Cress, our brains are wired to see patterns in everything. Rock formations. Paint splotches. The random folds of bark in an old tree. We look for patterns in everything we see, finding ears and eyes and mouths and noses. Anything can look like a face if you stare at it long enough, like the people who found Jesus in a slice of burned toast. But if Cress thought Eric looked like Billy, too, that meant I wasn't imagining it.

"His nose definitely matches," she said. "See how stubby it is?"

"Yeah. And his smile."

Cress ran a few more searches on the library computer, looking for better pictures of Billy, but only

a couple popped up—the school photo and another one that was fuzzy, like the photographer zoomed in on a picture taken from far away.

"I guess his family wasn't into taking pictures," she said.

"Or they all got destroyed in a fire."

She rolled her eyes. "Not everything is a disaster, you know."

"I know."

"I mean, other than your hair."

I smacked her arm and she laughed, but I did take a second to redo my ponytail. It was still all lumpy on the top. Some people have a talent for things like hair and clothes, but my skills lie more in stubbornness and determination.

After school, I made the world's easiest lemon pie from a box of instant filling and one of Mom's frozen piecrusts. She always makes two at a time and sticks one in the freezer for later. She thought it was sweet that I was making a pie for my new friend. I wasn't about to tell her that it was only an excuse to go over there and spy on him.

While the pie set in the fridge, I tried to knock off some homework. Miss Rivera had given us a thick packet of worksheets for the Living Museum, and it wasn't the kind of stuff I could copy from Cress's packet, either. It was all personal questions about people we admired and history we wanted to explore. I got the first page done and felt like I needed a nap, so I helped Mom get dinner ready instead—broccoli-potato soup with slices of crunchy baguette.

Mom had a shift at the hospital that night, so we ate as soon as Stan walked through the door. That way she had plenty of time to put her feet up. By then, the pie had to be ready, so it was all I could do to sit still while Mom and Stan ate and talked about boring everyday stuff.

"Did you finish the big project you were working on?" Mom asked Stan.

"Almost," he said. "I might have to go in on Saturday night to oversee the conversion. We were planning to leave the rollout to the office in India, but they're having problems with their network, so we might have too much data loss."

Mom made a sympathetic noise, and I tried not to moan into my soup. I have nothing against computers, but Stan made them sound about as fun as watching paint dry.

"I have an extra night off this week," Mom said. "Friday."

"Maybe you'd like to join us on Saturday?" Stan looked at me. "What did we decide? Disco bowling or the nature center's river walk?"

I was so focused on shoveling in my soup as fast as possible that I couldn't remember for a second. "Sorry. The river walk, I think?"

Mom smiled. "That sounds lovely, but I'll leave it to you two. It'll be nice to catch up on my shows while you're out." She stood and stretched. "I'm going to put my feet up for a bit."

"I'm going to take that pie over," I said, slurping the last of my soup.

"I'll come with you," Stan offered. He glanced at Mom. "As long as you don't mind."

"Go right ahead. I'll enjoy the peace and quiet."

She kissed him on the cheek and I tried not to pace as he straightened up the kitchen and took forever lacing up his sneakers—seriously, how long does it take to tie shoes? I must have been staring pretty hard because Stan cleared his throat and smiled sheepishly at me, which sent a stab of guilt through my heart. He was being nice. He didn't know that I needed to get to Eric's trailer ASAP.

Or why.

Finally, we headed out, this time leaving Frankie behind. She watched us go with big sad eyes, but tonight,

I needed all my focus. Cress agreeing with me about the similarities between Eric and Billy had made things more serious. If Eric really was Billy Holcomb, then he was lying to everyone about who he was. You don't change your name and hair color for nothing.

Cress said the reason our brains sort images into patterns is a matter of survival. Brains that recognize threats stay alive. The ones that don't get eaten. I wasn't freaking out. My brain was simply doing what it had evolved to do.

I pumped hard on the way to the Jessups' while Stan coasted along, admiring the breeze and the tiger lilies blooming in neighbors' yards while I tried not to explode from impatience.

"Is this pie for your new friend?" he asked. "Your mom said you've been hanging out."

Oh my God. Mom was talking about boys with *Stan.* "Yeah. I guess."

"Are you . . . do you, um . . ." Stan searched for the words, stumbling like he was playing pig-pickin' charades. "Are you just friends?"

I nodded. No way on earth was I talking about boys with Stan.

Once we reached the Jessups' place, I had a different problem: what to do with Stan while I went to see Eric.

Stan didn't need to know what I was up to. "I'm going to drop this off real quick," I said, untying the pie box from my handlebars. "You don't have to wait for me."

"I don't mind waiting," Stan said, which made me feel bad for ditching him. When I hesitated, he added, "It's okay. I'll keep an eye out for shooting stars."

While Stan waited by the road, I crept through the woods, careful not to snag any booby traps. There were more of those cracked bowls out by the trailer, like decorations in a strange outdoor living room. The fading sunlight caught on the metallic cracks, making them gleam. I walked up to the trailer slowly, checking for clues that weren't there and wishing I had a better plan.

The door flew open and Eric popped out of the trailer like he spent all day looking out the windows, waiting for me to come by. He was wearing jeans and a faded blue sweatshirt with *Carolina* written across the front. There was a little triangle-shaped tear next to the second *a*. "Hey," I said, glad to see him alive but also wanting to shout, *"I know who you are and I'm here to save you!"* Only that would sound totally nuts. Even with Cress agreeing, there was still a big part of me that knew I could be wrong. That I was going to let everyone down again.

That I was following the same old pattern—one that didn't do me any favors.

"I made you another pie," I said, lifting the box. "It's lemon."

He brightened. "I love lemon."

I lifted the lid, but instead of looking awesome, the whipped topping had melted into a sad puddle of marshmallow. "Dang. I should've used Cool Whip."

Eric swiped his finger through the mess. "Mmm! Tastes good to me." He started walking toward the trailer and I followed after him.

"Why weren't you at school today?" I asked.

"I had somewhere else to be."

"Did you have to go to the doctor? Or the dentist? I hate getting my teeth cleaned."

He looked at me like I was acting weird.

Because I was.

It was ridiculous, me acting like a junior detective, but from what I could tell, me and Cress were the only ones who had any idea that Eric might really be Billy Holcomb. It was up to me to do something about it, even if I felt ludicrous for trying.

"So, I was wondering. Y'all came from Asheville, right? Did you grow up there, or somewhere else? Like maybe somewhere out east?" I asked.

Eric's eyes widened.

I could feel the truth hovering in the air between us for a long, slow minute. Then something rustled in the woods and Stan popped out from behind a tree with his skinny arms held out for balance.

"There you are," he said. "I got worried."

I spotted the twine strung between the trees a split second before he reached it.

"Stan, don't!"

But before Stan could understand what I was saying, his foot hit the trigger and down he went, squealing like a stuck pig.

12

THAT AGAIN

Now, I said before that Stan is a good guy, a great guy even. Because he is. But the one thing he is *not* is scary. To begin with, Stan is skinny as a swamp reed. He wears glasses. He sniffs every once in a while, like he's always on the edge of a cold. Flopping around in a booby trap, he looked about as harmless as a baby bird that had fallen out of its nest, but that didn't stop Kelsey from racing out of the trailer like her hair was on fire, waving a frying pan.

"Get away from him!" she screamed, swinging the pan in Stan's direction. When she reached Eric, she flung her arm in front of him, herding him back.

"Stop grabbing me," Eric shouted.

"Would you listen to me for *once*," she shouted back.

Meanwhile, Stan's arms and legs flailed, his limbs caught up in an old fishing net that had been strung over the shallow pit of Eric's booby trap.

"It's okay," I said, stepping in front of Stan. "He's my stepdad."

It felt weird to call Stan that. I hadn't introduced him to many people since he and Mom got married. Usually I called him "Stan."

Kelsey blinked. "You're that girl."

"Maddy," I said. "Maddy Gaines. Eric's friend? We just came over to visit."

She lowered the frying pan, but her grip was still white-knuckled.

Stan finally freed his arms from the tangle of netting and sat up. The sides of the pit only came up to his waist.

"Hello," he said from the ground. He got to his feet, brushed off his khakis, and extended a hand. "I'm Stan Wachowski. Pleased to meet you."

Kelsey gave Stan a quick nod, ignoring his out-stretched hand. He shifted his hand toward Eric, who flinched. Stan let his hand drop. "Sorry for barging in. I was checking on Maddy."

"And I was bringing you a pie," I said.

Eric held up the pie box, and Kelsey glared at it like it was booby-trapped, too.

"It's lemon," Eric said, but she only glared harder.

"How many times have I got to tell you?" she said. "You don't need to build them traps."

"It's your fault we need them," Eric shot back.

All the fire went out of Kelsey at once. Eric's face closed up like a book, and an awkward silence settled over us.

If I set aside their hair color, Kelsey and Eric looked an awful lot alike. Same stubby nose, same blue eyes, but their ears were different. Kelsey's didn't stick out. Her black hair was pulled back into a ponytail, and on second look, it was definitely dyed. A dark blue tattoo peeked out from under the sleeve of her green Lucky T-shirt.

Before I could figure out what to say next, Diesel Jessup's father charged around the trailer with a shotgun in his hands. He ran in front of Kelsey and Eric and started to lift the gun.

"John, it's me!" Stan shouted, and recognition lit in Mr. Jessup's eyes.

He lowered the gun and bent over his knees, his breath coming in heavy pants. "Dang it, Stan. I just about shot you." He glanced at Kelsey. "You okay?"

She had her arm around Eric, who actually let her hold him for a second before he shook her off and moved away. "We're fine," Kelsey said.

Mr. Jessup blew out a long breath. "Good Lord. I thought Bob was out here. About gave me a heart attack." He lifted his hat to wipe his bald head. "Sorry about that, Stan."

"It's okay," Stan said a little weakly, his eyes still fixed on the gun.

Mr. Jessup's eyes settled on me. "Well, hello there, Maddy Gaines. It's been a while since we've seen you."

"I've been busy," I said, leaving out the part about Diesel being a jerk. "Are they your family or something?" I said, looking between Mr. Jessup and Kelsey.

Kelsey's eyes went wide, but Mr. Jessup gave me a big ol' smile. "Naw, we're old friends is all. We go way back."

"Maybe you know my wife, then?" Stan said to Kelsey. "Sarah Wachowski. Formerly Gaines. Her parents have since moved down to Florida, but she went to Northern High School."

"Never heard of her," Kelsey said, her eyes hard. "I think you'd best be on your way."

"Of course." Stan nodded. "Sorry again for the confusion."

Mr. Jessup tipped his hat. "I'll see you around, Stan. Tell Sarah I said hello."

"Sorry about the trap," Eric said.

Stan waved him off. "No worries. Really."

"It's not like it worked or anything," I joked.

Eric gave me that sly grin of his. "Good thing I didn't put the spikes in yet."

Stan and I were quiet as we walked back to the road. It was late enough that the stars were coming out, and my mind buzzed with everything that had happened. I needed to get home and call Cress so we could talk in private. Hopefully she'd be willing to help me figure it all out.

"Well, that was interesting," Stan said as we climbed on our bikes.

"You can say that again."

"'That again,'" he said, and I groaned.

Stan may be a good guy, but he is very, very far from cool.

13

THE BIRDS AND THE BEES

I woke up to the sound of singing. Mom was sitting on the edge of my bed, running her nails over my back while she hummed "You Are My Sunshine." Dad used to sing it, too, but my favorite was when they sang it together. Their voices were a perfect match.

I peeked at Dad's picture on my nightstand, and a pang of loneliness struck my heart.

Mom hadn't finished yet, but I rolled over and wiped the sweaty, tangled hair out of my eyes.

"We need to get you a haircut," she said as she finger-raked my bangs, which wouldn't stay in place. I don't have the kind of hair that takes orders. "I can't remember when your hair's been this long." She sat back, revealing a church-shaped box on the bed next to her.

87

"You got Munchkins?"

"Of course."

She opened the box and we each grabbed a small, round doughnut—chocolate glazed for me and cinnamon sugar for her. The doughnut was still crispy on the outside, the icing flaky and fresh. I inhaled the first one and reached for another as Mom moved Croc out of the way.

"I heard you had quite the adventure last night," she said. "You didn't mind that Stan came along, did you?"

"No."

"Good. He thought maybe you did."

Did I? When he showed up and fell into Eric's booby trap, yes. But other than that, I wasn't sure. "I thought he was gonna faint when Mr. Jessup ran up with his gun."

Mom nodded grimly. "Well, Stan isn't so used to seeing guns. I assured him that John's more interested in shooting copperheads than people. He said you didn't bat an eye."

I smiled, surprised by the compliment. "Well, it *was* a little scary."

"I can imagine." Mom looked off, thinking. "I'll have to check in with John and make sure everything's okay."

That was just like Mom. She always wanted to help people. I think that's why she became a nurse. One time when I was little, she threw a hunk of firewood at a black snake in our yard to make it drop a baby bunny. The snake spit that rabbit out so fast. I still remember what Mom looked like, standing there in her nursing uniform, flinging logs over her head.

"Hey, Mom?"

"Mm-hmm?"

"Did you know a girl named Kelsey in high school?"

"I don't think so."

"She's staying with Eric in the Jessups' trailer."

Mom gave me a soft smile. "Oh, right. Stan said she was quite the character. No, I can't say I know her. Why?" There it was—a hint of concern in her eyes.

"She sounds like she's from around here."

"She might be. I don't know everyone in town."

"What about someone named Bob? Mr. Jessup was worried he was there."

Mom made a face. "What is this about exactly?"

"Nothing. Never mind." I stuffed another doughnut in my mouth and acted cool.

Mom watched me chew. "You know, when I got my driver's license, Grandpa gave me this old Ford he had sitting in the garage for years. That truck was the most unreliable thing. Broke down every week, and when I couldn't afford to fix it, John worked on it for free."

"He did?"

"Yep. That's how we met. I drove over to visit your dad at the trailer park and the truck died in his drive-way, so he called John to help me out. John's family didn't have much, but he and his dad used to fix up old junkers and sell them. You know John put himself through college that way? He's a good man, same as your father was."

Her eyes got all soft and shiny. "Anywho, I hope you're having fun with Stan on your adventures. I know he is."

She smiled, and I felt plain rotten inside, remembering how I'd wished that Stan hadn't even come along for the bike ride the night before. He *was* trying.

"The planetarium was fun."

"Good," Mom said. "That's great to hear. I know I've said it before, but I want you to be happy, Mads. There's been a lot of change around here, and . . . well, there are going to be some more changes. You're growing up, and Stan and I—"

"Mom. This isn't a sex talk, is it? Because we already did that in school."

One day in fifth grade they sent the girls to one room and the boys to another room and gave us puberty talks. It was awful. First they started talking about body changes, and then about the birds and the bees. At the end they gave us tiny folded pamphlets that were different for each group and included all kinds of tips on going through *the change*. We spent the rest of the day trying to steal each other's pamphlets, even though I think everyone was equally as horrified to find out what was in the other group's pamphlet as to never know at all.

"Oh my goodness," Mom said. "It did sound like that, didn't it?" She rubbed her hands over her face, her eyes heavy and tired. "I guess you're almost right. Listen, how would you feel about adding to our family?" She looked at me in a way that said this was a lot more serious than adopting a puppy or something like that. Which could only mean—

"Like a baby?"

She nodded. "Like a baby."

A *baby*. Mom and Stan's baby. My throat got tight just thinking about it. I mean, I knew this could happen now that they were married, but hearing that word made it so *real*.

"It's okay if you're not excited about the idea," Mom said. "You might even feel angry or sad. That's normal. You can tell me and I won't get mad. Scout's honor." She smiled and held up three fingers, which was an inside joke. I got thrown out of the Brownies for not being Scout material. I had Becky Thorpe's little brother sit on

91

my stadium seat pad to check it for size and sewed it to his shorts. Really, I was just mad that we weren't out in the woods lighting fires.

I swallowed hard against the lump that was growing in my throat. I should be happy about a baby. I should want a little brother or sister.

Mom squeezed my hand. "Change is hard for me, too. Do you remember how many paint swatches I got for the living room before we finally finished it?"

"A million?"

"Try *two* million. Your father would've known what he wanted in a heartbeat, but I'm not built like he was. It takes me a while to get used to a new idea. This is a big one, but I think a little brother or sister could be fun for you. Can you imagine Stan changing diapers?"

She wanted me to laugh, but I couldn't, though I did imagine little diaper-changing diagrams written in Stan's precise block letters, like an assembly line for poop emergencies.

"Oh, honey." Mom wrapped her arms around me. "Are we okay?"

I nodded against her shoulder and she said, "Remember, we're in this together, Mads. You and me. No matter what happens, I'll always be here for you."

She hugged me tight, and I felt how much she wanted

me to be okay. I wasn't a little kid anymore. I was eleven. Almost twelve. Mom needed to know I wasn't going to freak out. She needed to know she could trust me. I pushed that awful emptiness aside and looked into her eyes.

"I love you, honey," she said.

"I know."

"I know you know, but it's my job to say it as many times as you need to hear it." She smiled, plucked a powdered doughnut from the box, and booped my nose.

I smiled back and did the same thing to her.

14

ALSO KNOWN AS BOB

On the bus, Cress's eyes were sleepy and red. She yawned as I slid into our seat and handed me a purple binder. Inside, the pages were covered in brightly colored Post-it notes. Her neat cursive filled the squares—all notes about Billy Holcomb.

"Wow, you did all of this last night?"

She nodded. "After I finished half of my packet."

"You did *half* already?"

"Yeah. I need to decide who I'm going to be so I can put my name on the list." Miss Rivera had posted a list in the library with slots to sign up for a Living Museum character. There could only be one of each person. I still had no idea who I wanted to be.

I smoothed my hand over Cress's pages. She had

organized the evidence into neat rows with guesses as to what each clue meant. Like Eric's name: Eric Smith. Was that his real name? And his super-blond hair. Either he was a true blond or we'd spot dark roots one day. Cress had listed both possibilities with an empty check box next to each. There were boxes for every other detail about him: his height, his weight, his eye color, and what matched or didn't match according to the missing-person report and our guesses.

Then there was the news I'd told Cress last night—how Mr. Jessup was so worried about someone named Bob being down by the trailer that he ran up with a gun.

"Listen," Cress said. "I have to show you something. Promise you won't freak out."

"I won't freak out."

"Swear on the blood oath."

"I swear on the blood oath, okay?"

"Look at Billy's dad's name," Cress said, pointing at an article she'd printed out and highlighted, right next to her handwritten notes.

"Robert Holcomb," I read aloud.

"Also known as *Bob*."

"Dirty wipes! Do you think that's the Bob Mr. Jessup was talking about?"

"Might be. These are facts. My mom says people lie all the time, but facts do not lie."

Spelled out like that, it did look like more than a wild guess. Mr. Jessup could've been talking about Billy's *dad*. Which meant there was a connection between Eric and Billy.

"What if this is real?" I whispered. "What if Eric really is Billy Holcomb?"

I imagined calling the sheriff's office. The police flooding our neighborhood, surrounding the trailer with searchlights, sirens blaring, like a scene out of a movie. Then I imagined them telling me that Eric Smith wasn't Billy Holcomb and how Sheriff Dobbs would look at me with that awful mixture of pity and sadness in his eyes.

"Relax, Mads," Cress said. "There have to be a million dads named Robert who go by 'Bob.' We need evidence that it's really him—like a photo, or a birth certificate. Something real, that's on paper. A case lives or dies on the evidence."

Cress was right. We needed evidence.

Grown-ups never believe kids until they've seen a thing with their own eyes.

I let out a long, slow breath. "Mom and Stan want to have a baby."

"Wait, what?" Cress said, her eyes wide.

"It's weird, right? I mean, they're old."

"They're not that old. Not like grandparents old."

I bumped her arm. "Ew, gross!"

Cress laughed as the bus pulled into the school parking lot. "Speaking of gross, Mom said I'm getting my braces next week. I'm going to look like such a dork."

"No you won't. Lots of kids have braces."

"It's *metal*. In my *mouth*. And rubber bands! Mia says the boys made fun of her every day. They called her Brace Face and said she had germs."

"Who cares what boys think? If they say anything, I'll shut them up."

Cress smiled as the bus pulled into our spot and jerked to a stop. We stood up to join the line of kids filing down the aisle, but before we could get out, Diesel cut us off.

"My daddy said you were on our property again," he said to me.

"So?"

"So, take a hint."

"You're the one who can't take a hint." I knew being smart would only make him mad, but I couldn't help myself. He looked so silly trying to threaten me. Like a big, goofy bull.

His nostrils flared.

"Come on, Maddy," Cress whispered. "Give him a break."

And in that split second, I saw something I hadn't noticed before: While Cress was talking to me, Diesel was looking at Cress, and she was kind of smiling, looking down like she was shy of him. Something shifted in my gut—a deep, gross feeling, like falling off my bike.

"Come on, Cress. Let's go," I said, pulling her past Diesel.

I tried not to notice when she glanced back at him.

That afternoon, I tried to work on my Living Museum packet at home. First I searched all the historical figures on Miss Rivera's list, but nothing really sparked. Each person was interesting and they'd all done amazing things, but when I tried to write about any of them, I started thinking about Dad and wondering if anyone would ever study him this way.

Where were the books that recorded ordinary people?

Every year in November, we celebrate Dad's birthday. Mom always makes a cake and we spend the day telling stories about him. My favorite is the one about how they met. Mom was in high school, working the funnel-cake booth at the county fair when one of the ride operators walked up. He wanted a funnel cake without powdered sugar, but he didn't have any money. He said he'd take a reject if she had it. Mom rolled her eyes because people were always asking for free funnel cakes. Who doesn't like crunchy fried dough? But there was something in Dad's dimpled smile that changed her mind, a kindness that made her heart swirl.

"He didn't look hungry," she said. "He looked hopeful."

On Mom's break, she brought him a plain funnel cake on a paper plate. It wasn't even burned, which made her stomach feel like it was full of butterflies. Dad took the funnel cake and asked her to follow him. She didn't know why she went—maybe it was that hope written in his dimples—but she followed him to the back of the Whirl-A-Gig, and when they got there, Dad crouched down and lifted up a scrap of corrugated metal. Beneath the metal was a family of baby raccoons. They looked like little bandits in hiding.

Mom took one look at Dad feeding those babies, and that was it. She was in love.

"How do you know if you love someone?" I'd asked her, when she first told me about Stan. Love seemed like some kind of mysterious force that traveled invisibly between people. It didn't seem right that you couldn't see it or control it, and that it could strike at any time.

"I ask myself if I can live without this person," Mom said. "If the answer is no, it's love. That's how I felt the

99

first time I saw you. Your eyes were squeezed shut, like this world was too much to look at. I brought your little face right up to mine, and finally, you cracked your eyes open. I never thought I could love someone as much as I loved your father, but then you came along and showed me different. I've been learning from you ever since."

I knew that love. I felt it every day, in her hugs and her kisses, but it seemed to me that love was just as likely to break a person in half as it was to save them. Every morning with Stan at our breakfast table was a morning Dad missed.

"You can fall in love, but your heart can get broken, too," I said.

"Love can do both," Mom said. "It hurts and it heals. You have to risk one to gain the other. But I have never regretted loving someone."

"Not even Dad?"

She'd cradled my face in her hands. "Especially not Dad. He gave me you."

15

APRIL FOOLS

om made sunny-side-up eggs for April Fools' Day, only when Stan cut into his, it was really a canned peach sitting in a pile of plain yogurt. He got Mom back, though. When she tried to scoop the cereal he'd poured for her, the milk was frozen. You wouldn't think that breakfast pranks could make people laugh until they cried, but for us they did.

Stan and I spent the afternoon on the paddle boats at the science center, trying not to spin in circles. Afterward, I biked over to Eric's. This time I brought Frankie with me. She was thrilled to see Eric, but not as thrilled as he was to see her.

"Hey, Frankie. Hey, girl," he said as she licked him all over his face and arms. Frankie wagged as he scratched her ears. His fingers were dirty, the tips stained red from clay.

"You been digging?" I asked.

He looked up from loving Frankie to smirk at me. "Maybe."

"What for?"

"Come see." He took off toward the cemetery, and me and Frankie followed.

We wove through the trees, ducking under tulip poplar branches full of baby red leaves. The treetops were filling in, and the air was sweet with honeysuckle. All around us, bugs buzzed and goldfinches tittered, busy building nests for the eggs they would lay soon.

When we got to the Roach family cemetery, I couldn't believe my eyes. Branches were piled all along the edges of the graveyard in a giant V. We stopped at the point of the V, and my foot twanged against something. I whipped around right in time to see a log swinging at my head, and hit the ground with a scream, only to watch the log swing to a gentle stop above us, held back by a rope.

Eric clapped his hand against his scrawny leg and laughed. "April Fools'!"

I gave him the stink eye while Frankie furiously licked my cheek. "That was *not* funny."

"Was too. You should've seen the look on your face!"

I stood up, brushing off the dirt and leaves. "You're fired. Right, Frankie?"

She wagged at me, and Eric's smile faded. "Aw, come on. You're too short for this trap. It never would've hit you. I wanted to test it, and I figured it was April Fools'. . . . "

I looked up at the log, which hung a good two feet above my head.

"Don't be mad," he said, looking down at the ground like I'd broken his fool heart. It sure was tempting to give him a real hard time, but I had questions to ask and answers to find.

"Where'd you learn how to do all this booby-trap stuff, anyway?"

"YouTube. This is a screen. Anyone who comes through here will get funneled into the trap. See how the branches block the way?"

I did see. And it looked plain wrong to me. "You can't pile all this mess in a cemetery."

Eric shrugged. "What do they care? They're dead."

"It's disrespectful. Just because they're dead doesn't mean they don't care. Their ghosts might care. *I* care." His lips curved into a frown, and I thought of how Kelsey had yelled at him about the booby traps. If he shut me out, I wasn't going to get any answers. "We could move it over," I said. "That way it would cover more of the woods, too."

He considered what I'd said and nodded in agreement.

I looped Frankie's leash over a stump and we got to work, carrying branches to make piles, bending saplings and tying them down to make a fence. I pulled up some briars and draped them over the branches so it looked like a natural, overgrown stretch of woods. Afterward, Eric helped me collect bluets and star grass to decorate the graves, which only seemed right.

When we finished, it looked like the Roach family had been there, keeping company. The Christ Baptist Church does the same thing every summer on Decoration Day, when families visit the graves and share a meal with their loved ones. I like the idea so much that every year on June 2, Mom and I picnic in the field where we spread Dad's ashes.

I knelt to run my fingers over a tombstone. You could read the date 1863 at the top, but the letters didn't make much sense.

Eric crouched next to me. "I think it says 'Ophelia.'" He dragged my finger in a circle so I could feel the *O*. By the time we'd traced the whole name, my cheeks were on fire.

I stood up, feeling like I'd been turned inside out.

"What exactly are you building all these traps for, anyway? You trying to catch something?"

"No. They're just in case."

"In case of what? A bear?"

He busied himself with a length of twine, tying and untying a knot. "My dad."

My breath caught. "Is that who Mr. Jessup was talking about the other day?"

"Yeah."

Eric rubbed at his arm, and I noticed angry red scars along his inner elbow where the flesh is tender. Dread pooled in my gut. "Did he do that to you?"

Eric yanked the sleeve of his Carolina sweatshirt down. "My dad isn't a nice guy," he said. Then he turned away and sat down with his back against a giant oak tree.

Watching the way his shoulders slumped, I didn't care about those notes Cress and I had made about Billy Holcomb. Maybe I could be Eric's friend. Then the part of me that needed answers stirred, and I knew I wouldn't be able to let it go—but I could still be there for him.

I sat down next to him, and Frankie sprawled out between us, looking for a belly rub.

"I'm sorry," I said. Eric stayed quiet, and in a way I was glad. Sitting close like that, I started listening to the sound of my own breath, trying not to be too loud.

Every once in a while, I stole a peek at him. Was it my imagination, or were there dark roots coming in along his scalp?

I'd finally gotten up the courage to ask when he said, "Is it true your daddy drowned?"

All the wind rushed out of me.

I shut my eyes, and behind my eyelids I saw that blue-gray color of the beach house, and the sky, and the ocean water when it runs fast and deep. The currents are invisible. They're hidden far below the surface, and by the time you find them, it's too late.

A crashing sound built in my ears.

At first I thought I was hearing the ocean again, but then Frankie started growling, the black fur along her spine standing up like porcupine quills.

"Someone's coming," Eric said.

We scrambled to our feet.

Standing outside the screen was Kelsey, looking madder than a bag of wasps.

16

FLUFFERNUTTER

This one time last year, Mom caught me spying on our neighbors, the Davises. Their garage was crammed with stacks and stacks of old newspapers, and I was sure their house was going to burn down because that's a huge fire hazard. My plan was to sneak in and clean the newspapers out an armload at a time, but when I stood up from my hiding spot in the bushes to run inside the garage, Mom was standing in their driveway. She said I had to come home that very second.

I didn't argue. My whole body tingled with the shock of being caught. That's how I felt when Kelsey found me and Eric out in those woods.

"I told you to stay by the trailer," she said, grabbing Eric's arm. "You can't wander around like this."

"Let go," he said, twisting out of her grip.

"Jessamyn said you ran off after school. Where've you been all this time?"

"Here."

"Doing what?"

"Hanging out. Like *normal* people." He stubbed his toe into the ground.

Her glare softened. "Right. Okay." She let out a breath. "Look, I'm sorry for yelling—"

"*And* grabbing me."

"—and grabbing you," she repeated, with a tiny smile. "You gave me a scare is all. Don't run off like that again, okay?"

"Okay," Eric said, "but Maddy's staying for dinner."

I started to beg pardon, but Kelsey fixed an eye on me and said, "Well. I guess you've got to eat." She didn't smile or ask if it was okay with my parents, but I texted Mom anyway.

"Have fun with your friend," Mom texted back, which made me blush. I reminded myself that I was *not* the type of girl who had crushes on boys. Boys were decent friend material if you picked the right one, but I was not interested in losing my mind over one of them.

This was strictly a snooping opportunity.

At the door to the trailer, I stopped to brush off Frankie's paws the way Mom did at our door, to be polite. Once we were inside, Frankie strolled straight into the living room and plopped down, bracing her back against the La-Z-Boy chair with a satisfied grunt.

In the kitchen, Eric grabbed two glasses of soda and sat at the little table with the mismatched chairs while I watched Kelsey move around the kitchen and wondered what we would eat. She opened a cupboard, and without even washing her hands, dug out slices of white bread, a jar of peanut butter, and a jar of Marshmallow Fluff.

"Plain or toasted?" she asked.

"Plain is fine," I said, even though I had no idea what she was making.

She slathered a layer of peanut butter on one slice of bread and a layer of marshmallow on the other. Then she slapped them together and handed me the sandwich, no plate. I half expected her to say, "April Fools'!"

But she didn't.

"Is this a joke?" I asked.

"It's a fluffernutter," Eric said. "Haven't you had one?"

"No."

"Time's a-wastin', then," Kelsey said, so I sucked it up

and took a bite. Salty sweetness coated my tongue. As I chewed, the white bread melted away like it was made of air. The sandwich was surprising but satisfying, like that first lick of ice cream on a hot summer day.

I must've smiled because Eric said, "It's the best, right?"

Kelsey handed him a sandwich and he tore into it like he hadn't eaten in a week. She laughed. "He can't get enough to eat these days. Been growin' like a weed, haven't you?"

Eric smiled a little bit, and my mind raced, because that was the answer to one of our questions: Eric was a lot taller than Billy Holcomb . . . but it had been six whole months. He might've just *grown.*

While Eric ate every last crumb of his fluffernutter and licked his fingers clean, I sat there thinking I should ask him if his daddy's full name was Robert, but with Kelsey there, I couldn't get the words past my lips.

Kelsey put the bread and jars back in their cupboard and sat down next to us. Then she dumped out a paper bag full of broken pottery bits and began to sort them. The pieces were terra-cotta on one side and blue glaze on the other. Their edges looked sharp enough to cut hair, but Kelsey handled them with ease.

"What do you think?" she asked Eric.

For once, he didn't make a face or get mad. "It'll be a good one."

She smiled, the first full smile I'd seen on her, and it lit up her whole face.

"She breaks them on purpose," Eric said. He passed me one of the bowls with metal cracks, and I realized what Kelsey was doing. She was fitting the pieces back together.

"I learned the technique while I was . . . away," she said. "It's called *kintsugi*. You use lacquer with metal to fix up the pots. It honors the history of the piece." She moved her hands as she talked, and I noticed splotches of paint and smudges on her skin that I'd missed before.

"Where did you go?" I asked.

Kelsey's hands went still. She cleared her throat and threw a quick glance at Eric. "I think maybe it's time for you to get home now, Maddy."

My face went hot. "Can I use your bathroom first?"

She nodded, and I walked down the hall as slowly as possible, trying to catch a glimpse through the bedroom doors, but all I saw were clothes and beds. Normal stuff. I didn't even know what I was looking for. It didn't help that Kelsey was showing me this other side of herself, acting all nice and feeding me fluffernutters and smiling and stuff.

In the bathroom, I spent a minute finger-combing my hair into something resembling order and wishing I had an ounce of my mother's beauty before I washed my hands and looked for a towel to dry them. That's when I noticed a plastic bag hanging on the door handle. It was a regular grocery bag, thin and white, which let the ghost of what was inside show through: a tall, narrow box with the close-up picture of a woman.

My heart kicked up a notch.

I pulled the bag open. Inside were two boxes of hair dye: one platinum blond, one ebony.

For a second, it felt like all the air had been sucked out of the room.

"Fluffernutter," I whispered as my heart raced.

I dug my phone out of my pocket, but when I went to dial 911, my fingers froze.

My gut said these boxes mattered the way a trail of hoofprints matters when you're tracking deer, but I still didn't have any *proof* that Eric was Billy Holcomb. And no proof that he was in trouble. I couldn't call Sheriff Dobbs. He'd laugh at me, or worse, call Mom about it.

I left the bag on the doorknob and walked into the living room feeling numb. Kelsey was laughing over something, but her smile faded when she saw me standing there.

"Everything okay?" she asked as Eric twisted around to look at me, too.

Two strangers, staring back at me.

"I have to go." I waved my phone like Mom had texted, when really I felt like I couldn't breathe. It was ridiculous to be scared of them, but I was.

"I'll come with you," Eric said.

Kelsey watched us leave, her eyes wary, her mouth tense. The idea that she might go to the bathroom and figure out what I'd seen had me rushing through the woods.

"Is something wrong?" Eric asked as he struggled to keep up with me and Frankie, who bounded along like this was a fun game of chase.

"I'm fine," I said, even though I wasn't.

What did it mean, if Eric's hair was fake? He might just like trying different hair colors, but why would Kelsey dye her hair, too?

With a start, I realized that Kelsey was probably not even her real name.

The world tilted, like some kind of April Fools' joke gone horribly wrong.

When we finally burst free of the woods, I took off running. Frankie leaped after me, excited to race even if she didn't know why. We got to the ditch by the side of the road, and it took me a minute to process what I saw. I hadn't bothered to hide my bike in the neighbor's holly bushes. With everything that was going on, the territory wars had begun to feel silly, but I was kidding myself if I thought Diesel Jessup was going to ignore my trespassing forever.

The ditch where I'd left my bike was empty.

In its place was a ransom note.

17

BLACKMAIL

The note was messy, with words crossed out and smudges of dirt here and there, like someone had gripped the paper with muddy hands and scribbled the message in the dark.

Cress read it three times before she sorted it out.

"You are guilty of trespassing," she read as the bus pulled out of my subdivision. "Bring a six-pack of Kool-Aid Jammers or you will never see your bike again." We were sitting far enough away from Diesel not to be overheard, but close enough for me to shoot him dirty looks.

Cress chewed her lip, thinking. "That doesn't sound like Diesel."

"Of course it does. It's blackmail!"

"Well, you did trespass on their property when you went in the trailer, right?"

I groaned. Sometimes Cress is too honest. This was the kind of situation where you took your best friend's side, even if what she said was wrong.

"You should talk to him," Cress said. "Maybe this is a mistake."

"Diesel doesn't listen to anybody. It's like talking to a tree stump."

Cress frowned. "He's smart, you know. He helped his dad fix our garage when that tree fell on it over winter break. He's actually kind of nice."

That warm, sick feeling crawled over me again. "Do you like him or something?"

"No," Cress said, but she wouldn't look me in the eyes.

Instead, she opened the binder with our facts about Billy Holcomb. "I looked up that hair dye. It's permanent. So they only need to do it again when the roots are growing out." She'd copied this information onto neat Post-it notes in the binder. "It's a good clue—"

"But it's not proof," I finished.

"No." Cress ran her tongue over her new braces, making a weird sucking noise. "My cheeks feel like hamburger," she said with a groan.

"Does it hurt?"

"It feels like my teeth are going to explode. And when I eat, all the food sticks in there. I have to floss every single tooth like three times and it takes forever." She hung her head and I pressed my arm against hers. "Plus, I finally decided on Harriet Tubman, but Becky Thorpe already signed up for her, and she's not even black!"

"Forget Becky. You'll find someone else. And your project will be the best. It always is."

Cress nodded, her lips pressed together to hide her braces, and I ignored the whisper of worry in my mind that said time was ticking down and I was no closer to figuring out who I was going to be, either.

On our way off the bus, Eric and Diesel caught up to us. Eric gave me a little wave while Diesel strolled by like he didn't see me at all, much less like he was black-mailing me for parking my bike on his lawn. As they went down the steps, Diesel even had the nerve to glance back at Cress and smile.

My stomach sank when she smiled back.

"Maybe *you* should talk to Diesel," I said.

Cress's mouth popped open. "Why me?"

"You're the one who likes him."

As soon as I said it, I knew I shouldn't have. "Sorry," I said. "I don't know why I'm being such a jerk."

"It's okay," Cress said, even though I knew it wasn't.

I'd watched the video of Billy Holcomb's dad pleading for information enough times to know it by heart, but I watched it again when I got to the library. Mr. Holcomb stepped up to the microphones, his jaw tight, and read his speech from a paper in halting words.

"Whoever knows where Billy is, whoever may be with him—this is a plea for you to bring him home. The Fayetteville PD, the State Highway Patrol, and the FBI are all looking for you. You may have good intentions, but I'm sure you realize this situation is bigger than you anticipated. Turn Billy over and we will not pursue you. I'll take him back with no questions asked. Please let this nightmare be over and bring my boy home."

The whole time, his hands are shaking. He looks so sad. His face is tan and handsome, his beard a mix of black and gray. It must have been early in the morning because the sun is in his eyes. At the end of the video, he puts his sunglasses on and turns away. I watched the video again and thought about how scary it would be to be kidnapped. Was that what had happened? Had Billy been kidnapped? My brain sorted the pieces over and over, but I still didn't have the answers. I still didn't know how to help.

"Hello, Maddy," Miss Rivera said from behind me, and I jumped half out of my chair. "Researching your Living Museum project, I hope?" She wore a green-and-white shirt that said *Librarian, because Book Wizard isn't an official title.*

I laughed. "I like your shirt."

"Thank you." Her eyes went to my screen. "What's this you're watching?"

I started to say it was nothing, but Miss Rivera was too sharp to buy that. And besides, maybe she could help me—as long as she didn't think I was freaking out over nothing. She was always so helpful, she might actually give me a chance.

"I'm trying to find more information about Billy Holcomb. He's the boy who went missing last fall."

"Oh, I remember that."

"That's his dad on the video."

"The poor man," she said. "What exactly are you looking for and why?"

I took a breath. "I'm trying to find out what happened."

"Why?"

"To keep other kids safe?"

Miss Rivera's eyes softened in sympathy. "That's thoughtful of you. I can help you find some resources—as

119

long as you promise to get me a name for the Living Museum this week?"

I nodded quickly.

"Okay. Well, I'd say your best bet is local newspapers. They are the ones most likely to have unique information, though they might be hard to find because their distribution will be limited. Most things are on the internet, but it takes skill to find accurate information."

She slid the keyboard her way. "What matters most are your search terms. Then you need to make sure each source is legitimate." She showed me the different catalogs and websites that would be good places to start. "Promise me you'll get to work on your project? It's so special when the students are all in costume and the families come to walk through the halls."

I remembered the Living Museum packet mentioning something about giving a speech to guests. That wasn't the part that bothered me, though.

"I'll try," I said.

18

TIME TRAVELERS

The problem with change is that you're never ready for it. Even when you know a change is on the way, it still sneaks up on you somehow. I guess that's why most changes usually feel bad. No matter how much you prepare for them, they still catch you by surprise.

A week had passed and I was still stewing over the ransom for my bike when Stan found me lying in a patch of sun in our backyard, tossing a pinecone into the air. Every once in a while, I'd throw it, and Frankie would take off at a sprint to fetch it back.

"Mind if I join you?" Stan asked.

I could have said something mean like "it's a free world," but he wasn't the one I was mad at. I was surprised to find that in addition to Diesel, I was also mad at Cress. Diesel had stolen my bike, but she kept smiling at him. Plus, despite using Miss Rivera's research tips, I still hadn't found any evidence to prove Eric was Billy Holcomb. And then Eric had shown up at school with blue hair. *Blue.* Like he was only changing the color for fun, which made me think he wasn't in trouble at all. Maybe I was wrong about him. Maybe I was wrong about everything.

Stan settled onto the grass next to me, or at least he tried to. First he crossed his legs. Then he stretched them out. Finally, he flopped back like a normal human, pulled off his glasses, and wiped them with the bottom of his red checked shirt one lens at a time.

"It's nice back here," he said, admiring Dad's field. The flowers were coming to life. Yellow forsythia glowed in the sun, mixed with masses of white anemones. Dark clumps of daisies and coneflowers were on their way. Soon the whole field would be blooming.

"My dad planted it." Of course Stan probably already knew that, but I felt this need to say Dad's name, to keep him present. The barrier loomed in my mind.

"He did an amazing job," Stan said, really taking the time to admire the field before turning to me. "Any ideas about what we should do next weekend?"

"Well, it *is* Easter." I was hoping we could skip the

whole awkward hangout for once, but Stan took my words the wrong way.

"Ah! An egg hunt?"

"I think I'm too old for that."

"Oh. Right. Of course." He shook his head. "I keep forgetting you're almost a teenager."

Was I? I didn't feel that grown up, especially when my mind filled with evil thoughts as I watched Cress and Diesel smiling at each other at school.

"I hope that glare isn't for me," Stan said. "I promise I come in peace. Actually, I hoped we could talk about the idea your mom mentioned. About adding to our family."

A baby. I swallowed hard.

Stan looked as uncomfortable as I felt, but he forged on. "So, the thing is . . . well, you and your mom—and your dad—you were a family a long time before you and I met."

I kept my body perfectly still. It felt like if I moved, the world might explode.

"And, well, the thing is—" Stan's eyes moved from me to his little red notebook, which had appeared from out of nowhere. Did he really need to have that thing with him *all* the time?

"I'd like to ask for your blessing," he said. "I know that sounds strange, but it's important to me that you're on board with adding to our family, the same as you were with your mom and me getting married. I would never want to do anything to hurt you, Maddy."

He stopped talking, his eyes fixed on the field. My body floated above us, my arms and legs lost in time. There are moments when it feels like the world is changing too fast for me to keep up, and everything tilts. It's like catching a glimpse behind the curtains of the universe. Suddenly the past, the present, and the future are all mixed up.

Stan had been around for a whole year before he and Mom got married, but there was still so much I didn't know about him. Maybe it was being in Dad's field or maybe it was how everything seemed to be changing, but suddenly I was full of questions.

"Have you ever been in love before?" I asked. "Before Mom, I mean?"

Stan's pale cheeks pinked up. "Well. Yes, I suppose I was in love once or twice, but I never felt at home until I met your mom—and you."

The barrier threatened, but I pushed back.

"What happened with those other people?"

"Well, I guess it didn't work out." He gave a clipped laugh. "Or maybe it did?"

He looked at me with so much hope in his eyes that I felt a little guilty for prying. It wasn't Stan's fault things were all mixed up. He could have ended up with some other

family, but he didn't. For all we knew, there was some other universe out there where Dad was still alive and Stan was not. I just wished I felt like I'd ended up in the right one.

The first time I met Stan was at the Greek Festival in Greensboro. Fifth grade had started the week before, and I was excited to roam the festival lawn. It was always crowded, but in a good way. People gathered under gigantic white tents to buy arts and crafts, eat mountains of food, and dance in huge circles. The music alone was enough to make me smile.

Mom and I were in line for food when a tall, clean-shaven white man in a dress shirt walked up. He said hello to Mom like he knew her already, then introduced himself to me, which was the way it always went when we were out. Mom knew everyone because of her job as a labor-and-delivery nurse—we liked to joke about how many babies she "had" each night—but people usually moved on after they chatted for a few minutes.

Stan didn't leave.

By the time we got to the front of the line, he'd told me all about how computers talk to each other and how one day they would be able to think for themselves.

When it was finally our turn to order, I'd never been

more grateful to see the food ladies with their spatulas and serving spoons. We bought a plate of pastitsio, which is like lasagna but better, and skewers of pork souvlaki with pitas and stuffed grape leaves on the side. We also grabbed baklava and hen's nests for dessert, which are so delicious they make me wish I knew how to make them so I could have them all the time. Stan helped carry our trays to a table where he'd held some chairs for us. Seats go fast at the festival. You have to stake out your place early if you want to hear the music. As we settled in, Stan and Mom exchanged a smiley, googly-eyed glance, and I got this funny feeling in my stomach, like they had a secret I wasn't in on.

While we ate, Stan kept spilling stuff—the saltshaker, his drink, his plastic fork. Looking back now, I guess he was nervous. At the time I thought he was a weirdo who talked too much about computers. I did my best not to encourage him, but the trouble with not talking is that it's hard not to think about all the horrible things that could happen. Like how the old lady across from us could choke on her lamb shank. Or how the little kids under the table could get flattened. Or how the tent could collapse and crush us all. I don't want to think these thoughts, but sometimes they fill my mind like a million tiny aphids sucking a tomato plant dry.

After a while, the music changed and the dance

troupe performed. At the end, they invited the audience members to come up and join a giant dance circle with arms linked.

"Maybe we should try it?" Mom said.

She took my hand, and Stan's, too.

In the dance circle at the Greek Festival, the music goes faster and faster and the circle moves quicker and quicker until you're all leaning on each other as you kick and jump. We went so fast it felt like I was falling . . . until I really was falling. Stan tripped and pulled me and Mom down with him, along with a bunch of other people, but the strange thing was, no one got upset. No one got hurt. Everybody just laughed and lifted each other up and started dancing again.

Sitting in the field with Stan, I realized I'd forgotten how strange it was to meet him that first time, and how quickly I'd gotten used to having him around. Sure, it was weird to think about him and Mom having a baby, but everything new is weird at first.

I picked a rock out of the grass and held it up. "Is this a friend of yours?"

He laughed. "I'm never going to live that down, am I?"

"Nope."

We both laughed, and for a moment I felt this lightness, like gravity had given way.

Stan plucked a buttercup and twirled it between his fingers. "Did you know that ninety percent of the material that makes plants grow comes from the air, not the ground?"

My brows rose. "I thought you didn't like nature."

"I don't have a lot of experience with it, but that doesn't mean I don't like it. I enjoy learning new things."

I looked at the field and imagined the air full of invisible plant food.

"Water, air, and energy," Stan said. "Those are the key ingredients for life."

I thought about how the air around us seemed empty, but it wasn't. How life depends on things we cannot see. And how maybe we are all time travelers, trying to find our way.

Even Stan.

"I give you my blessing or whatever," I said before I chickened out.

I wasn't sure that I believed what I was saying, but I knew Mom would've wanted me to be brave, even if I was scared. Plus, she says that babies are actually pretty adorable when they aren't pooping, and she's probably right about that.

19

THE LIST

For the life of me, I couldn't figure out why Eric was friends with Diesel. As we walked into school the day before Easter break, they laughed and bumped into each other like best friends, which would have made sense if they were anything alike, but they weren't. Diesel was a jerk who stole other people's bikes. Eric made you fluffernutters and petted your dog.

He was *nice.*

Eric glanced at me as I turned for the library, and when our eyes met, I got that funny feeling in my stomach again. I knew what that meant, but I was determined not to develop a crush. Look at how Cress was acting. It was like she'd forgotten she ever hated Diesel in the first place. With Eric, it was complicated. Now that we were friends, it didn't feel right to keep spying on him, but it was going to take more than blue hair to make me give up.

On *America's Most Wanted*, they said that a lot of times it's regular people who discover the fact that breaks a case, like a note in a diary or an address in a pants pocket. People are messy. They leave clues everywhere. It can be hard to see them if you aren't looking, but the truth is already there, buried under everything else.

I just had to keep looking.

When I got to the library, Miss Rivera helped me put together a fresh list of newspapers in the Fayetteville area, where Billy Holcomb had disappeared. If she thought that was strange, she didn't say so. Miss Rivera always says that what and how we read is our choice, as long as we're reading.

"Now, about your Living Museum project—"

"I know. I need to pick someone."

"Yes, you do. How about Anne Frank? Or maybe Marie Curie? She won a Nobel Prize in Physics. You could make your own radioactive notebook to go along with your outfit."

It shouldn't have mattered, but none of those names sparked anything in me. It's like I was waiting to hear the one name I knew I never would.

"What about Georgia O'Keeffe?" Miss Rivera said. "She was an American artist who painted mountains, skulls, and flowers. Her simplified style was groundbreaking and very cool."

I still didn't feel a spark, but I nodded anyway. "Okay. I'll take her."

"Excellent," Miss Rivera said. She walked away, past a new library sign in the shape of a cell phone that said *Books, the Original Handheld Device!* I only had time to look at a couple of websites on her list before the homeroom bell rang. On the way to class, I saw Diesel in the hall and felt this urge to shout at him for stealing my bike, but he probably would've laughed at me. Instead of making a scene, I put my eyes on the millions of tiny pebbles in the floor and promised myself I would get back at him later.

Usually, art class was my favorite. I love making things, drawing things, and figuring them out, but I'd been avoiding making my model for the Living Museum. Everyone else had already started. I couldn't stall any longer, but this wasn't a matter of figuring it out. This was about deciding to actually do something, even if it was scary to do it.

Our art teacher had all kinds of materials to choose from. Clay, Popsicle sticks, foil, Styrofoam balls, recyclables that kids had brought in from home, and my favorite, papier-mâché.

Depending on their historical figure, kids were making all kinds of props, like masks or hats or swords with blunt edges. I hadn't looked up Georgia O'Keeffe yet, but I knew she was an artist, and an artist would have paintbrushes or an easel or something like that. Instead of making any of those things, though, my fingers rolled the papier-mâché into a tube like a telescope, only shorter and with a knob on top. A site level. It's what surveyors use to measure distances and heights. When I finished the model, it would need a stand. I wasn't sure if we still had one in our attic or if I would need to build that, too, but my hands knew what they wanted to make.

20

SISTER STUFF

I kept waiting for Cress to go back to normal, but something had changed between us. I couldn't see exactly how, but I could feel it, like a tiny splinter working its way into my heart.

"I don't want to get stuck babysitting again," she said as we rattled our way home on the bus. "Mom says we should be grateful to spend Easter with our cousins, but it's no fun. Mia never helps. We're at church all day and there are no cell phones allowed."

"Do they have an egg hunt?"

"Yeah, but I have to help hide the eggs now that I'm twelve."

"That stinks." Cress is six months older than me, but sometimes it feels like more than that.

She nudged my shoulder. "You know what they say, eleven is heaven!"

"No one says that," I said, and we both cracked up.

The bus turned onto Cress's street, which is in one of the newer subdivisions that have popped up around the middle school, where huge fields used to hold black-and-white cows. Her house is at least twice as big as ours, but not in a stuck-up way like Diesel's.

"You'll help me with my model when I get back, right?" Cress said. "I need to make a miniature *Friendship 7* to go with my Katherine Johnson costume. I asked my dad for help and he stared at me like I was speaking French."

"Doesn't your dad actually speak French?"

She jabbed my arm. "You know what I mean! My dad is hopeless. If it isn't something to do with Mia's soccer team, he can't handle it. I think he wishes we were boys."

Sometimes, when Cress and Mia are fighting and I ask what it's about, Cress shakes her head and says, "Sister stuff." I've wondered what that's like, being a sister. Cress is the closest thing I've ever had to one. But sometime soon I'll be a *real* big sister, which is so weird. By the time I'm Mia's age, my little brother or sister could be five years old.

"I'll help you with the spaceship," I said. "We'll use cardboard and papier-mâché."

"Listen," Cress said. "I'm not kidding."

"I believe you. You're the most serious person I know."

She jabbed at my arm again, but I dodged her. "You better text me while I'm gone," she said. "*Especially* if you find anything new about you-know-who."

"I will. Wait, I brought you a surprise." I unzipped my bag and pulled Croc from inside. His purple face was all squished. "I thought you might want some company on your trip."

For a split second, Cress's smile fell. Like she was surprised, but not in a good way. "It's okay," she said. "I wouldn't want to lose him in Atlanta."

"You never lose anything."

"Well, maybe I'm done taking Croc on trips. He's kind of a little-kid thing, you know?"

The world tilted. Things were changing too fast again. We used to fight over custody of Croc, and now Cress was done with him, just like that?

"Keep it together while I'm gone," Cress said as she hugged me good-bye.

She was only leaving for a long weekend, but it felt like more than that.

It felt like she was leaving me behind.

When I went back to school after Dad died, everyone stopped talking to me. I mean everyone. Even Diesel stopped poking fun at me on the bus. It wasn't because they were being nice. It was because I didn't have a dad anymore. It was like I'd turned invisible.

Right after Halloween, a new fourth grader showed up at school. She wore a khaki skirt and a white button-down with short sleeves that glowed against her rich brown skin. Her hair was braided with white beads, and she had a gold-and-green turtle bracelet that matched her gold-and-green turtle earrings. Later, I found out her family had moved to North Carolina from Georgia, but her father was from Trinidad, where Cress spends part of every summer. That's where she got the jewelry. She also had a wide, swinging accent that the other kids made fun of. I thought it was mean how they mimicked her, but kids will make fun of anything.

Back then, I used to bring a book to lunch so I had something to do while the other kids talked and laughed. I was into this story called *Tuck Everlasting* about these people who drank from a magical spring and lived forever. The weird thing was, they didn't like living forever. The boys always stayed the same age, and their parents were

always their parents, and nothing ever changed. While part of me thought they were strange for feeling that way, I could also see how it would stink to stay a kid forever. *Especially* if you were in middle school.

Mom always sent an extra cookie with my lunch for sharing, but I usually ate it myself and squished the foil wrapper into different shapes. If you rub a lump of foil against the edge of a table, you can shape it into something cool, like hearts or stars. I collected the foil shapes in my book bag until Mom found them and started asking questions. After that I recycled them.

On the new girl's second day, she brought a book to lunch, too. From then on, we sat together at lunch, reading quietly, until one day when she passed me her bag of barbecue chips. I passed her one of my cookies, and that was it.

We clicked.

It's like we both saw something in each other that we didn't see in other people, only that something isn't anything you can actually *see*. It's more like something you just know.

21

SEEING RED

On holiday weekends there is no homework, so after I helped Mom dust and vacuum because she was sick of seeing dog-hair tumbleweeds everywhere, I took Frankie for a walk. I told myself it was a normal walk and that I was not going over to the Jessups' or anything like that, but that's exactly where I ended up.

As usual, I couldn't help ogling their gigantic house. The rounded windows on the castle section were lit up. I always thought that would be the coolest place to have a bedroom. Of course that would mean sharing a house with Diesel, so maybe Mr. Jessup could build a new bedroom for me at my house, a slightly smaller one, with a rounded section for my bed.

Frankie pulled me toward their lawn, so I stopped

and let her take a bathroom break. We kept doggie bags clipped to the leash in case of this exact situation. After I bagged her poop, she bounded around me like she'd accomplished something great.

"You're a good girl," I said as she wagged her butt.

I was about to get walking again when I heard a strange noise. It wasn't quite a laugh, more like the snort you make when you're trying not to giggle at something really funny.

I studied the house more carefully.

There was a blanket fort on the Jessups' front porch, and Devin and Donny were hiding in it. They burst out laughing when I spotted them.

"Doo-doo, doo-doo, you touched doo-doo!" they chanted.

I am way too old to get upset about something like that, but I felt my aggravation rise.

As Devin and Donny laughed at me, I started swinging Frankie's poop bag in circles.

Swoop, swoop, swoop.

I hadn't made up my mind about exactly what I was going to do until Diesel stepped outside and said, "What are you dorks going on about?"

There is something that happens to your body when rage flushes through you. It's a prickly feeling, like every part of you is coming awake to the wrongness of the world, all at once. All I could think was that Diesel was the one who'd taken away the pond and stolen my bike, and now he was trying to take Cress from me, too.

They call it "seeing red" in the movies. It's when you get so angry that the emotion takes over your body. For me, it meant winging that bag of dog poop at Diesel's big block head.

He ducked, and the poop bag hit the Jessups' front door with a sickening, squishy thud.

"That's for stealing my bike!" I shouted.

I'd expected Diesel to mouth off, or even throw something back at me, but he just stood there looking stunned. We stared at each other, him holding the screen door wide, the poop bag lying at his feet like the saddest goody bag ever, and me, feeling downright sick to my stomach. Part of me wished I hadn't done it, but I had. And then, like a coward, I ran.

After I do something embarrassing, I can't sleep. I lie there in bed, thinking about whatever I did over and over, wishing I could change it. I was lying in bed not sleeping and thinking about throwing that poop bag when I heard our porch boards creak in a way that was not the wind.

For a second I lay there frozen, clutching Croc to my chest. Then I drummed up the guts to crawl to the end of my bed and press my face against the cool window glass.

As I watched, a kid-size person hopped from the porch onto the pebbled path that led to the driveway. I could tell from the shape of his big block head that it was Diesel Jessup. He stopped halfway up the path and turned around. For a second, I swear he looked right into my eyes. I felt sick about what I'd done all over again, even though he totally deserved what he'd gotten for stealing my bike. In fact, he was probably out for revenge.

My blood started thrumming, thinking of what he might have done to our house.

When I was sure he'd left, I snuck downstairs and went outside.

My bike was sitting there on the porch, waiting for me.

22

A TROJAN HORSE

I didn't know what had come over Diesel, but I wasn't giving him more credit than he deserved. Maybe he felt guilty, or maybe that poop bag had done the trick. For all I knew, my bike was covered in poison ivy.

Miss Rivera once told us the story of how the Greeks gave the Trojans a giant horse sculpture as a gift, but the sculpture was actually full of Greek soldiers who came out at night and attacked. The Trojan horse was a trick. My bike might be a trick, too.

First thing Friday morning, I scrubbed the entire thing with dish soap just to be sure. Our family is not religious, so Good Friday is like any other Friday for us, only with school off. Meanwhile, Stan went to work and Mom rested, catching up on sleep after her night shift.

She was already in bed when I woke up, but she'd left Munchkins on the table.

One of my favorite things to do when Mom is asleep is watch those talk shows she says will rot my brain. The people on them are so interesting. They have these weird problems that would embarrass most people, but instead of covering them up, they go on national television to talk about them. I can't decide if they're brave or foolish.

When I got tired of watching strangers argue, I spent a few minutes looking up Georgia O'Keeffe. She painted all kinds of flowers and rosy pictures of the desert with lots of bleached white bones, but her clean, swoopy lines made everything look a lot simpler than it is in real life.

I bookmarked a few websites and pulled out the list of newspapers from Miss Rivera.

It turns out there are eighteen different online newspapers that cover Fayetteville, North Carolina. Most of them had the same information I knew by heart: Billy's description, his last known sighting, and what happened the day he disappeared. Everyone seemed to have the same information said different ways. Sometimes, there were pictures with the articles. I'd gotten so used to seeing that one school photo of Billy that I skipped right past the photo of his dad at first. I think my brain assumed it was some random guy in an internet ad until the sunglasses registered. They were the same ones Billy's dad had worn in the news conference, the one where he spoke into the cameras, squinting into the sun.

I scrolled back.

That's when I saw Billy's dad was wearing a Carolina-blue sweatshirt. The thing about Carolina blue is that it's a very specific color. You can't mistake it for any other shade of blue. It's not cobalt or baby blue or cerulean, which means "sky blue" in Latin, according to Cress. Carolina blue is the color of a sunny day, when there isn't a single cloud in the sky, not even those wispy ones the airplanes leave behind. Carolina blue is the color of summer and vacations and the ocean. Maybe for that reason, it's not a color I like very much.

In the photo, the sweatshirt is still bright blue and the man is still young. His hair is dark, his skin tan, and his teeth white. But none of that matters. What matters is that his Carolina sweatshirt has a little triangular tear next to the second *a*. Exactly like the one Eric always wore.

It's weird when you find something you've been looking for but that you didn't quite believe was real. Staring at that picture of Billy Holcomb's dad was like seeing an actual photograph of the Easter Bunny. Real and not real at the same time.

In the photo, Billy's dad seems like a nice guy. This time, looking at his smiling face, all I could see were those angry red scars on the inside of Eric's arm. If Eric was Billy, this was the man who'd hurt him. I'd felt bad for Billy's father. When I first saw his video, I'd cried. But that wasn't who he really was. That video was a lie, like the Trojan horse.

My stomach twisted, sick with truth.

I scrolled all the way to the top of the article and found an update that had been added to the text a few weeks after Billy went missing.

"UPDATE: Billy has been located and is safe, according to officials."

My breath caught.

If Billy had been found, what was he doing in our town? And why was he hiding who he was? Maybe he was in trouble again. Or maybe he'd never gotten out of trouble to begin with. It wouldn't be the first time officials had gotten something wrong.

All I knew was that this sweatshirt was a match.

It was proof.

I'd spent so much time worrying about being wrong that I hadn't thought much about what it would feel like to be right. Maybe that was because I'd gotten to know Eric, and even though I had the proof right in front of me, I didn't want him to be in trouble.

I wanted him to be safe.

If I called the sheriff's office, what would happen?

Would I be taken seriously, or would this proof be ignored, too?

I tried to think like Sheriff Dobbs. He wanted facts. He wanted to know beyond a shadow of a doubt. The goose bumps along my arms told me this photo was exactly what he wanted.

WHAT IS

23

I don't know what to do with this picture, so I call Cress. She doesn't pick up the first time. The second time, she answers but she is somewhere so loud that she can't hear me, even when I shout into the phone. Then there are a bunch of scuffling noises and the call goes dead. I text her that I have HUGE NEWS, but she doesn't text back, so I'm pretty sure her phone got taken away.

I think about calling the sheriff's office, but something is holding me back.

I guess it's the fear that even if I'm right, the call will still go wrong somehow, and Sheriff Dobbs will show up at our house to talk with Mom about how messed up I am again. Or that if he does believe me, somehow it will be bad for Eric.

Eric who is really *Billy*.

In the end, I text Dad about what I found, give Croc a hug, and promise myself that I'll figure it out soon. I just need a little more time to think about it.

When I walk downstairs for lunch, Mom and Stan are laughing about something while she's slicing tomatoes. His arms are around her waist. They see me, and Stan moves away from Mom like that's what he'd planned to do all along, but I know it has more to do with me.

"Turkey okay?" Mom asks.

"Sounds good." I perch on a stool next to the island while her soft hands make quick work of my sandwich.

"Big plans for today?" she asks.

It's Saturday, time for me and Stan to hang out, but I am too distracted for goofing off.

I shrug, and Stan says, "I thought you might want to see the new kid movie that's out? The one with the dogs who run a day care?"

I do want to see the new kid movie, but right now all I hear is the word *kid*, and the way Cress said it when she turned me down about taking Croc, like anything for kids is bad. I don't want to grow up, but I don't want to be a little kid, either.

I swallow my bite of sandwich. "No thanks."

A wrinkle appears on Mom's brow. "You feeling okay?"

I shrug again.

Meanwhile, Stan has the paper out, looking for something to do. He has no idea. None at all. I know he can't possibly understand what's on my mind if I haven't told him, but he just looks so ludicrous reading the paper while kids are out there being hurt.

"There's a new sculpture exhibit at the Arboretum," he says.

"No thanks."

"Roller skating?"

"Pass."

"I guess we could go for a bike ride?"

There must be something on my face that tells Mom I'm about to say something horrible, because she says, "Actually, I could use some help today. It's time to dye the eggs."

Stan raises his eyebrows. "Sure. Sounds fun."

Last year, Stan wasn't here when we dyed the eggs. He and Mom were a thing, but she still kept all of our traditions just for us. I filled the rainbow assortment of egg-shaped cups with warm water and stirred the little dye tablets until they dissolved like we always did.

This year, Stan suggests we use vinegar.

"Vinegar is acidic," he says. "Food coloring only works in an acid environment, so if we make the water more acidic with vinegar, we should get brighter colors."

I snort. "Is there anything you don't know?"

"Actually, it's written right here on the package," Stan says.

I can feel the barrier forming between us, like a shield wrapped tightly around my heart. All the while we dye eggs, I can't shake my aggravation. It feels like everything Stan does is on purpose, to irritate me. Which can't be true, but I shouldn't even be sitting in my kitchen making pretty Easter eggs when Eric is out there, right now, waiting for someone to help him.

Waiting on *me* to do something about it.

"I found something," I blurt out as Stan completes a perfect gradient on an egg.

"Something wrong with your egg?" Mom asks.

"No, my egg's fine."

Now they're both staring at me, and I've already said there's nothing wrong with my egg, which looks like a lemon, exactly the way I wanted, so I can't make that excuse.

My throat gets dry.

If I say this, will Mom think I'm overreacting again?

I fix my eyes on my egg and brace for *concern.* "I found

this picture of Billy Holcomb's dad and he's wearing the same sweatshirt as that new kid, Eric. Plus I found hair dye in their trailer and this big wad of cash in their cookie jar. I think they might not be who they say they are. I think Eric might be Billy Holcomb, that boy who went missing last fall."

There is definitely concern on Mom's face now. "Mads."

My chest tightens. "I know it's him, Mom. The news said they found him, but what if he's hiding out here, pretending to be someone else?"

She shakes her head. "John said his visitors are friends from out of state."

"Eric told me they were from Asheville. Mr. Jessup's lying!"

Mom frowns. "John would never do that."

"I know it sounds ridiculous, but I think Eric is Billy Holcomb and I don't want you to say I'm overreacting again, because I'm not!"

Now she looks disappointed, like I am failing her.

I bury my face in my hands.

After a long silence, Stan says, "They did act a bit strange when we visited."

I look up. He's got his thinking face on.

"We shouldn't feed into her anxiety," Mom says

quietly, as though speaking softly will make it hurt less for me to hear it. I know I'm not supposed to blow things out of proportion, but this is different. This is *real*.

Stan makes a small noise of disagreement. "Actually, it's been proven that people with higher levels of anxiety are better at spotting trouble and reacting to it," he says in his Encyclopedia Stan way, which makes me want to hug him. "People with anxiety tend to have higher IQs, too, which makes sense, because evolution usually serves a purpose. All that aside, I would say that there was definitely something odd about the whole situation. Especially when John charged in with his shotgun. For a second there, I thought I was toast."

Mom looks momentarily dazed and says, "Thank you for sharing this with us, Maddy. Let me talk to John, okay? We'll make sure everything is all right and see if they need any help with anything. I'm sure everything is fine."

My stomach has been busy tying itself into knots, but when she smiles, it loosens.

Maybe this time will be different.

24

EASTER

Usually on Easter morning I go straight to Mom's room and jump on her bed to wake her up. It's tradition. This year, I don't fling the door open and run inside without asking. Instead, I knock and wait outside in my pajamas, another Easter tradition.

After a minute or so, Mom opens the door in her robe. Stan is behind her, yawning as he nestles his glasses into place. He's wearing sweats, which *technically* qualify as pajamas.

"Ready?" Mom asks.

I can't help smiling. Cress might call our tradition a little-kid thing, too, but I don't care. The egg hunt is one of my favorite things we do all year.

"On the count of three," Mom says.

"One, two, three, go!" It sounds different with Stan counting, too, but I dash downstairs ahead of them and start grabbing plastic Easter eggs. They are everywhere. Jammed between the couch cushions. Perched inside the lampshades. I collect as many as I can while Mom and Stan do the same thing. We all know how the eggs got there, but we don't say a thing.

Soon the eggs are harder to find.

"There should be forty-two," Mom calls out.

We count our hoards and discover we've already found them all, as well as all the Easter baskets. It goes a lot faster with three people hunting. We gather at the dining table and open our eggs to see what we got. I crush the coin count with nearly five dollars in quarters. There are chocolate eggs and malted-milk eggs and gumballs shaped like eggs.

Stan beams the whole time.

There's an Easter basket for him, too. It looks stiff and new, compared to my faded and battered basket with its broken twine poking out the sides. Watching Stan, I feel this weird mix of happiness and embarrassment. I'm careful not to look into his eyes so I don't feel one hundred percent awkward. It's easier if I pretend it's only me and Mom.

"I love you," I text Dad.

When our stomachs start growling for real food instead of chocolate and candy, Mom pops into the kitchen and comes back with our dyed eggs and a set of bowls.

"Grab the salt and pepper, would you, Maddy? Stan, we could use some juice, too."

Stan piles his candy into his basket and grabs our drinks while Mom and I get ready for the Easter egg battle. Once we're all seated at the dining table, we choose our eggs and prepare to battle. Each battle consists of one person holding their egg steady while the other person taps their egg against it. You have to tap pretty hard, until one of the eggshells cracks. That person loses. The winner goes on to play another round, until there is only one egg left.

Since Dad died, Mom and I have done multiple rounds and kept track of the score. This year, there is a third player, so there will be a champion again.

Stan catches on quickly. He takes forever selecting his egg, tapping them with his fingertips to test for strength. A thick shell with no cracks is critical for success. He wins his duel with Mom and so do I, which leaves me versus Stan for the final round.

"I hereby challenge you to a duel," he says, offering me the pointy end of his egg, which is where the shell is the strongest.

I tap my egg against his. Nothing happens.

"Is that all you've got?" he says.

I tap harder. Still nothing.

Mom claps, cheering us on.

I really smack our eggs together, and there's a crack.

"Cheezits." My egg has broken.

We peel the eggs and eat them with salt and pepper. My favorite is the egg white. I'm not the biggest fan of the yolks. They pile up on the edge of my plate.

"You going to eat those?" Stan asks.

When I shake my head, he rescues my abandoned egg yolks and eats them.

"I can't believe you like the yolks," I say. "They're so gross."

Mom gives me a look.

I raise arms in protest. "What? They taste like a fart in your mouth!"

Stan laughs hard, wiping at his eyes. "That would be the sulfur," he says. "Eggs are high in sulfur, but only certain people can really smell it."

That's twice in two days that he's defended me. A warm feeling fills me up. I think maybe it's more of the barrier melting away.

I turn to Mom. "Did you talk to Mr. Jessup?"

"I did. He said Kelsey and Eric are new to the area

and he's helping them get on their feet before they move into their own place. They're regular people who are down on their luck."

"But that picture—"

"Lots of people have Carolina sweatshirts," Mom says.

"But it's the same one! There's a tear by the second *a*. You have to call him back."

Mom sighs. "I hear you, Maddy, but I'm not hassling John on Easter."

Yes, it's Easter, but while we're hunting for candy and battling with eggshells, something bad could happen to Eric. Kelsey could take off with him. They could leave like Mr. Jessup said. Or Mr. Holcomb could find them. Mom isn't thinking of those things, though. She doesn't understand how important this picture is. And Cress still hasn't texted me back.

We use the leftover hard-boiled eggs to make deviled eggs for the pig pickin' happening later today. We have one every Easter, as well as the Fourth of July and Labor Day. The location rotates around the neighborhood. This time, it's in our court.

A pig pickin' isn't any old picnic. It's an all-day thing. The truck pulls up at ten in the morning, its brakes squealing, and the men from the neighborhood association wrestle the smoker to the ground. The pig will have already been cooking all night. After they unload the smoker, they set up tables in the middle of the court. Stan goes to help. I watch from my window as he walks up our long driveway to the cul-de-sac, which I can barely see thanks to the trees that are filling in. By the time May arrives, you won't be able to see our house from the road.

While I watch, this waiting feeling builds up inside me. It presses against my heart in a way that doesn't feel good, even though it's plenty familiar. It is the sense of impending doom.

That's when I remember what we forgot.

"Mom!" I run into the hall. "Mom! Mom!"

Mom's feet pad quickly to the base of the stairs. "What is it?" she says. "What's wrong?"

"We forgot to do safety checks."

She relaxes. "Okay. Let's do them now."

We start outside like usual, only I can hear the men in the court, and for some reason that gets under my skin. We check the dryer grate and the windows and trim a few branches off the forsythia bushes. Inside, we follow my checklist. Everything is safe and secure, but I don't feel better, and I know I won't until I decide what to do about that photo of Mr. Holcomb. No matter what Mom says, I know what I saw. That sweatshirt is the same one Eric has.

Mom brushes the bangs from my eyes and says, "Hey, bug. I know it was different this morning having Stan here for the egg hunt, but he loved it so much."

"I know."

Like I said, Stan is a great guy. I just can't get that picture of Robert Holcomb out of my mind. All this time, I'd thought he was a good guy, too.

"Can you help me with the potato salad?" Mom says. "I have to get the pies in the oven. Once everyone starts showing up, I won't get anything else done. I wonder if Jessamyn is bringing her brownies this year. Yum!"

I swallow hard. The party starts in a couple of hours.

Everyone comes to the pig pickin'. The whole neighborhood shows up, like it's some kind of giant family reunion. We stay up until the sun fades and the sky fills with bats and flying insects. Something magical happens when the adults are all busy eating and chatting. The kids roam wild. We play manhunt in other people's backyards and hop fences like it's totally normal. There are people we only see a few times a year at these parties, and that's it. But everyone always comes. Including the Jessups. And this year, maybe Eric and Kelsey, too.

161

25

BAG IN THE HOLE

Waiting is the worst. While the court fills up with people and laughter, I wait for Eric to show up. I'm so nervous, I keep dropping things. First Mom's napkin holder, then a platter of sweet corn. Luckily, the corn wasn't shucked, so the husks protect it.

Mom doesn't say another word about that photograph, but there's no way she's forgotten. She's staying cool, calm, and collected, even if that's not the way she feels inside. "Fake it till you make it," she says. I've tried pretending I'm okay, but I can never get my insides to match my outsides.

The Jessups finally arrive, but only their family, which makes me think Eric might not be coming. Part of me is relieved because I don't know if I'm ready to face him again, knowing what I know about him. Still, the part of me that needs him to be okay is worried.

I'm so distracted that I drift a little too close to Diesel while he's playing cornhole. He has a blue beanbag in his hand, and if he can't land it on the cornhole board, he won't get any points. He tosses the beanbag in his hand, making it flip each time. Flip, *thwap*. Flip, *thwap*.

Suddenly he stops and turns to me. "You here to thank me?"

"What for?"

"Your bike, duh."

I'm so confused, I don't say anything.

"Aw, you gave her bike back?" Devin says while Donny sticks his tongue out.

My face gets hot, and I remember to be mad. "Why would I thank you for giving back something you stole from me?"

Diesel's nostrils flare. "You really are clueless."

"I am not. I know that you're a big, mean jerk."

Diesel hefts the beanbag, and for a second I think he's going to nail me with it, but then he turns back to the cornhole board and tosses a perfect bag in the hole. That's worth three points and is darn near impossible to do. Diesel hoots as Devin and Donny start whining about how he always beats them, so I turn and walk away.

I got the last word in, but it feels like Diesel still won somehow. No matter how much I hate him, the fact that Cress likes him makes me wonder.

If he isn't evil, why would he steal my bike?

Most of the adults are gathered around the folding tables, which are chock-full of baked beans, macaroni salads, barbecue potato chips, coleslaw, and brownies. The air is smoky and sweet with pork. I grab a paper plate and load up, even though I'm not that hungry. I wish Cress was here. Even if she was nice to Diesel, at least we could hang out together.

While I'm nibbling on my pork sandwich, a scuffle breaks out on the other side of the folding tables. At first I think it's just a couple of guys goofing off the way grown-ups do at these things, putting each other in headlocks like they're in middle school again.

Then I hear Mr. Jessup shout.

He shoves some guy, who stumbles back, almost falling over. The guy straightens up and I get a major case of the creepy-crawlies. His dark hair is going gray. His skin is tan. He is the older, angrier version of the man in my photograph. He is the man from the TV.

Billy Holcomb's dad.

The air turns to sludge. I can't seem to catch my breath.

Right then, I hear Mom exclaim from behind me. She's facing our house, so she doesn't see the fight yet. I reach for her arm, but her attention is on something else.

"Shailene, is that you?" Mom says.

I turn around expecting to see another one of mom's labor-and-delivery patients, but instead it's Kelsey and Eric. Eric is a mess, his blue hair sweaty, his fingers and T-shirt red with mud. He must've been working on his booby traps again. Kelsey looks like a deer in headlights, ready to bolt. She's wearing those same ratty jean shorts and the green Lucky T-shirt. Her eyes meet mine. There is a zing between us, and I know that she knows that I *know*.

"It's you, isn't it?" Mom's voice is warm honey. "I didn't recognize you at first with that dark hair. It's me, Sarah. Sarah Gaines? Or rather, Evans when you knew me, Wachowski now. I haven't seen you in ages. What are you doing here?"

Kelsey hesitates. Eric is pale as a sheet, his eyes fixed on the men arguing behind us.

"Mom, that's him," I say, even though they can hear me, too.

She glances at me. "Who?"

"Eric—the boy I told you about. *Billy.*"

"Maddy—"

"They're the ones staying down at Mr. Jessup's trailer."

Mom looks at Kelsey and Eric in confusion. The shouting behind us grows louder, loud enough for Mom to notice. She cranes her neck. "What on earth—"

Kelsey leaps forward and my heart almost flies out of my chest, but all she does is catch Mom's hand so that Mom turns back. "Look, Sarah. We're in trouble. It's too complicated to explain right now, but we have to get out of here. If he sees us, we're done for."

Mom's mouth is a small round O.

She looks between me and Kelsey. "You're staying at John's place? He said he was helping out an old friend. I didn't realize—"

By the tables, Billy's dad shouts again. "You'd best tell me where they are, John! The police came to my house. They took my *guns*." His handsome face twists with rage. Mr. Jessup has him by his shirtfront. Other people try to pull them apart, but Mr. Jessup is too strong.

"There's nothing here for you, Bob," Mr. Jessup says. "Get out or we'll call the police."

"I don't care what some piece of paper says," Mr. Holcomb spits. "He's my son. *Mine*."

Mom watches this and nods slowly. "Maddy, take Shailene and—just take them to the house, will you? Quick now."

All I can think is that if Eric is Billy Holcomb, then Kelsey is the one who's hiding him, and the last thing I want is to take her to our house.

Mom bends so her face is close to mine. "I need you to trust me. Go. Now."

The fire in my chest burns so hot I can't think straight.

Stan rushes past us, toward the fight. The shouting gets louder.

"Maddy," Mom says. *"Now."*

Eric looks at me, his eyes wide enough to show straight through to his soul, and I know that even if I don't understand, we have to go. I take his hand and run, across the court, down our long driveway, to the safety of our house, hidden by the trees.

26

RIGHT AND WRONG

Inside, Eric and Kelsey retreat to the living room sofa while we wait for whatever comes next. I don't know what to say to them, so I don't say anything, but my thoughts are on fire. That was Billy Holcomb's dad in our court. Robert Holcomb, also known as *Bob*, who Mr. Jessup was so afraid of that he came running with his shotgun when he thought the guy was around.

All of this means that I'm right, but instead of relief, my stomach is filled with dread.

"I'm sorry I wanted to come here," Eric mutters, his voice choked.

Kelsey turns his chin. "Look at my face. Do I look mad?"

He shakes his head, and she pulls him to her side. Surprisingly, he lets her.

It feels like we're waiting outside the principal's office. All of us know someone is in trouble, but we're not sure who it is yet, and we don't want to find out.

Finally, after what feels like hours, Mom walks in, her hands full of aluminum pans and serving spoons. "Maddy, can you go help Stan with the rest of our things?"

I want to stay and hear what she says, but it's no time to argue.

I help Stan collect our stuff from the court along with Mr. Jessup, who comes inside to talk to Kelsey and Eric. They go out on the back deck so I can't hear what they're saying, but I can see them through the window as I wash dishes. Mr. Jessup talks first. Soon Kelsey starts crying. My pulse picks up, watching as she bends her head and weeps. Then Mr. Jessup does the most surprising thing— he wraps his arms around her and holds her tight. He pulls Eric into the hug, too, and they stand like that for a minute, until Kelsey pulls away.

Mr. Jessup says something else and she nods.

They come back into the house, looking as skittish as outdoor cats. "Thanks for the help, Sarah," Kelsey says in a flat, reluctant voice.

"Of course," Mom says. "I'm sorry I wasn't able to help sooner."

Mr. Jessup pulls his cap off and rubs a hand over his

bald head. "Sorry I wasn't straight with you, Sarah. I figured the fewer people knew, the better."

"It's okay. I understand." Mom waves for Kelsey to take a seat. "First things first, let's get you something to eat. You look like you're liable to fall out."

Kelsey glances at Mr. Jessup, who nods, and she and Eric take seats at our little breakfast table. Kelsey's eyes are tired and red. She rests her head in her hands. "I don't know what to do," she says. "We can't go back to the trailer now."

"That's easy," Mom says. "You're staying with us."

Kelsey starts crying again, and Eric stares at the table like he could bore a hole through it. I don't understand what's happening, or why Mom's acting like any of this is normal.

Because it's not.

Kelsey lied. She dyed Eric's hair. She gave him a new name. She *hid* him. Right?

I look to Stan for common sense, and he raises his hand, as if to say, *Wait.*

Mom sets two pork sandwiches in front of Eric and Kelsey and rests her hand on Kelsey's shoulder. "It's no bother, really. We don't have much space, but what we do have you are welcome to. I'll grab some sheets for the couch and we'll get you all set up. Now eat."

Kelsey takes a tiny bite of her sandwich and Mom nods in approval before she heads upstairs. Stan and Mr. Jessup start talking quietly, so I follow Mom. She's got her head in the linen closet, digging in the back for the sheets that Grandma Evans uses when she visits.

"Why are you being so nice to her?" I ask.

"When I talked to John yesterday, he told me he was helping out a family friend. I didn't realize who that was at the time. Now I do."

"What does it matter who she is? She lied to everyone."

"Yes, but—"

"Those aren't their real names, you know. His name is Billy. She *faked* their names."

Mom sighs and turns to give me a look. "It's my understanding that they've legally changed their names for their own protection."

"So she lied."

"Yes, but it's complicated, Mads."

"Doesn't seem complicated to me. She's *lying*."

Mom shoves the sheets. "She's his mother!"

I'm stunned silent.

Mom leaves the linens, takes my hands, and squeezes. "Mads. Listen to me. The woman you know as Kelsey, I knew her a long time ago. She's John's cousin and her real name is Shailene. She came to town once or twice when we were in high school, but I didn't know her well. I didn't even know she had a son, or that they were the ones staying at John's place."

"But she lied. She dyed his *hair*."

"Yes, and for good reason. I know you're scared for your friend, but things are not as simple as they may seem. Shailene's husband had his troubles and he took them out on her, and your friend, too. Bob hurt them very badly, for a very long time, and now they're trying to start a new life. John says they need our help, and I trust him."

I think of that video of Billy's dad. How he trembled. How he cried. But he is also the person who gave my friend those awful scars on his arms.

My head spins. Right and wrong are all mixed up.

"Sometimes life takes a bad turn," Mom says. "Some people have a hard time getting back on track. Shailene's made a lot of mistakes, but she's trying to fix that. I know you want your friend to be okay, but so does she. Can you try to understand that?"

I nod.

I may not trust Shailene, but I do trust Mom.

Mom breathes out real slow and looks me in the eye. "This is a lot for me to take in, too, but I promise everything will be okay, bug. For now, this is how we keep them safe. I need to ask you a favor, honey. You can't tell anyone they're here. Promise me."

This is not what I expected. I don't want to be right anymore.

I think about how Billy builds all those booby traps everywhere and what he said about his dad being mean. Mom says that every patient has a different birth because every person lives a different life, and I wonder exactly how different my life has been from Billy's. All I know is that he has been a friend to me, and now it is my turn to be a friend to him.

I make my promise.

27

BIG BADS

I'm eating a slice of pecan pie for breakfast when Billy pads into the kitchen in his sock feet and sits across the table from me. I tried to be quiet, but he must've heard me from the living room. His eyes are puffy and red, like he cried himself to sleep.

"Hey," he says.

"Hey."

It's weird, sitting here together.

Billy watches me take a bite of pecan pie, and his stomach growls loud enough to hear.

"Want some pie?" I ask. "We made way too much for the pig pickin'. If you don't help eat the leftovers, they'll just go bad."

He grins. "Sure."

While we eat, I watch Billy look around our kitchen. I've never thought of our house as small—we have two bedrooms and two bathrooms—but our kitchen really isn't much bigger than the one in the Jessups' trailer. Mom's baby tomato plants line the windowsill. Stan's fancy coffeemaker fills the counter. There are pictures of me on the fridge, including one of me and Dad at one of my birthdays, but suddenly I can't remember which one.

"What's that?" Billy asks. He's pointing at my list of safety checks.

I'm not sure what to say. I haven't had to explain the safety checks to anyone other than Cress. "It's a checklist of things to keep our house safe."

"Like a drill?"

"Sort of," I say, my stomach feeling queasy.

"We do drills, too. Sometimes we race to see how quick we can pack up and get out of the trailer." He smiles, and I wonder if he knows how weird this sounds. Who does something like that? No one, unless they're running from a Big Bad. Big Bads are the scary things you can't forget once the lights go out. The ones that keep you up at night. They can come from any part of life, real or imagined, but if you let them, they'll hunt you down. Like Mr. Holcomb.

"So. Kelsey's your mom, huh?"

"Yeah."

"And her real name is Shailene."

He shifts in his seat. "Yeah."

"And you're Billy. Billy Holcomb."

He nods, his eyes on his plate. "We changed our names. Shailene didn't want us drawing any attention so my dad wouldn't find out where we were."

Shailene. Not Mom.

"Was that your dad yesterday?"

"Yeah. That's him."

Billy glances up and I busy myself with my pie. I want to know what happened with his family and how they ended up here, but I'm not sure if I'm allowed to ask. Things must have been pretty bad to do what they did. To leave your home, change your name and your hair. Change your whole life. You wouldn't do that unless you *had* to.

The stairs creak, and Mom and Stan appear. "Good morning, sunshine," Mom says. She plants a kiss on top of my head. She gives Billy a warm pat, too.

Stan starts fussing with his fancy coffeemaker, which emits all kinds of grumbling and growling noises, like it's juicing the coffee from a stone.

Soon we hear a long, loud groan from the living room.

Shailene appears, her coal-black hair twisted every which way like she was tossing and turning all night.

Stan offers her a cup of coffee and she whispers her thanks.

"Did you get any sleep?" Mom asks.

"Some."

"Sorry about the couch. It's seen better days."

"Are you kidding?" Shailene says. "It's perfect. Thank you. Seriously. My brain wouldn't quit on me last night. I just want to get this over with."

"Get what over with?" I ask.

Mom and Stan exchange a glance, and Mom comes to sit by me. "We had a long talk last night, and Shailene filled us in on their situation. Because of what Bob did, a judge decided Billy should live with Shailene, but Billy's dad has had a hard time accepting that. Yesterday he violated a protection order. So, we're going to the sheriff's office today to report it."

"What's a protection order?"

"It's a court order issued by a judge to protect people. In this case, the protection order says Mr. Holcomb can't come near them, so you don't have to worry, okay?"

I look over at Shailene, whose hands are twisted in her lap. She doesn't look so scary anymore. She fixes a worried eye on Billy. "I don't think you should go to school today."

"That social worker lady says I have to."

"The school is well aware of the order of protection,"

Stan says. "They won't let Bob get to Billy there. He'll be safe."

Shailene doesn't look convinced.

"John will be here soon," Mom says. "Let us get the kids off to school safely, and in the meantime you're welcome to make use of the shower upstairs." A not-too-subtle hint. Or maybe it's only Mom's usual brand of kindness, because Shailene actually smiles.

Mom goes upstairs with Shailene to get her a towel and a washcloth, and probably shampoo, too. Selfishly, I hope she doesn't use up all of mine. The water comes on and stays on. Ten minutes later, I can't help thinking how Mom would be up there shouting at me for using up all the hot water, but this isn't business as usual. Instead the shower keeps running.

Meanwhile, Stan strikes up a cheerful conversation with Billy about the healing properties of pecans. A few minutes later, Stan hands us each a lunch, but Shailene doesn't reappear. The shower keeps running. She's still in there when Billy and I leave for school.

I barely step onto the bus and Cress shouts my name. "Mads! Mads! Check out my new earrings!" It's not only her earrings that are new—they're cute silver hoops—but her braids, too. She's had braids before, but this time there are red streaks woven through her hair. She looks like a rock star. When she smiles, her red braces bands match her new hair.

She stops smiling when she sees Billy follow me onto the bus.

I drop into the seat next to her, and luckily Billy keeps walking and doesn't say a thing.

Cress grabs my arm as soon as I sit down. "Atlanta was so fun this year!"

"Really?"

"*Yes.*" She flops back against the vinyl seat. "My cousins started a band in my aunt's garage. We got to see them play, and all these people came. It was so great. They're like a rock band, but with spoken word, too. Mia didn't even complain once. I wish you could've been there. You know what? Their videos are on YouTube. I'll text them to you."

She taps at her screen and my phone pings, but I'm too busy trying to figure out what looks so different about her all of a sudden, besides the hair and earrings. It's like her whole *being* has changed. Like she's stepped into her next self. Is that makeup on her eyelids?

"Anyway." She smiles. "What's the huge news you texted about? I wrote you back last night, but you didn't answer."

It feels like a million years since I sent that text. I'm not sure what to say. I don't want to lie to Cress, but I made my promise to Mom.

"It turned out to be nothing."

Cress's smile wavers. She glances back at Billy, her lip between her teeth. "What's going on with you two? Why did he get on at your stop?"

"He switched stops."

"Mads. Blood oath, remember?"

My face gets hot. I feel like I'm going to throw up, but it's not all my fault. Cress went away and she came back different. Or maybe she was different before she even left. She was the one who took Diesel's side over mine when she should have had my back.

"You broke the blood oath first," I say as heat courses through my body.

"What?"

"With Diesel. You kept talking to him after he stole my bike. You broke our blood oath over a boy." I know this is mean to say, but the words tumble out.

Cress's mouth falls open. "But he gave it back to you!"

"How do you know that?"

"He told me," she says, her voice soft. "You're totally wrong about him."

I want to shout at her, but Cress doesn't lie. Ever.

180

And I know that. But I don't like how she keeps taking Diesel's side, or that she talked to him before she talked to me. I get this gross feeling that even though Cress is back, she's still gone. Part of me is jealous, because I don't know how to do what she's doing. I don't know how to step forward into my next self.

"You know what," she says after a long minute of listening to the bus windows rattle, "I'm sorry I didn't call you back. I should have. Want to stay over on Friday?"

Relief floods through me.

"Okay," I say, and we both smile.

One of my scariest Big Bads is that Cress will ditch me one day. That kind of thing happens all the time in middle school. If you don't have the right hair or clothes, you're an instant target. Wear something ugly, and whispers and stares follow you all day. Say something wrong, and you'll hear about it until the end of time. This one time last fall, a girl I didn't even know punched me in the arm as she passed me on the stairs. For a second I thought I'd imagined it, but later on I found out that someone told her I had called her a loser. I didn't even *know* her. Now every time I see her in the halls I wonder if she'll hit me again. So far she just ignores me—but if that happened with Cress, I wouldn't know what to do.

181

28

STRANGERS

The weird thing about having strangers living at your house is that they're always there. Usually, visitors are only around for a meal or a party or a weekend, and then they leave. And you're glad. Because even when it's your best friend sleeping over, you aren't your normal self with strangers around, and that can get exhausting. Plus, they're always looking at your stuff and touching it.

Or at least Shailene does.

Wednesday after school, Billy and I snack on frozen grapes while Shailene goes through the living room, picking up our different family pictures and asking questions.

"This is your father, right?" she says, admiring Mom and Dad's wedding photo.

"Uh-huh."

"Handsome fella. I was sorry to hear about what happened to him. I wanted to send your mom a card, but I was short on cash." She frowns in real sympathy, which is surprising but nice. It's like she's shedding a few of her porcupine quills.

But she's still a stranger.

"Do you miss him?" she asks.

I nod. What kind of a question is that? Of course I miss him.

"You're lucky," she says. "You had someone real special in your life. Someone worth missing. Most people aren't like that. There aren't many people worth knowing at all, and most of them will leave you worse off than before you met them. Trust me, I know." She gives me this buddy-buddy smile, and I want to tell her there's no way I trust her. "How do you like the new guy?" she asks, making Stan's spectacles over her eyes with her fingers.

Normally I might laugh at that, but right now I'm annoyed. I don't like her talking about Dad and I don't like her talking about Stan.

"He's fine," I say.

"Yeah, he seems like it." Shailene sighs, rubbing her tired eyes. No one has said anything about what happened when they went to the police on Monday, but there's a mountain of paperwork on our dining room table that Mom warned us not to disturb.

Shailene leaves the pictures and walks over to us. "Sometimes I wish things had gone down differently for me, but then I wouldn't have this handsome fella, now, would I?"

She ruffles Billy's hair as his face goes red.

"Augh, Mom!"

Her face lights up. "What was that? What did you call me?"

"Nothing, *Shailene*," Billy says with a scowl.

"You'll crack one of these days," she says. "I can be patient."

This whole conversation is super awkward, so when Billy asks if he can go outside, and Shailene says he can so long as he "acts smart," I follow him into the garage.

Frankie jumps all over him the minute she sees him.

"Want to go for a bike ride?" I ask.

He shrugs. Then I remember he doesn't have a bike. "You could borrow Stan's bike."

"Are you sure?"

"It's okay. He won't mind."

Billy stares into Frankie's amber eyes and says, "Can Frankie come, too?"

"It's not easy to bike with her on the leash."

"I can handle it."

"Fine. It's your funeral."

We set out with him riding next to me, leading Frankie as I pedal slowly. We get to the main road and go a little faster, sticking close to the curb. After a few minutes of hills, we hit a flat stretch and Billy props his feet up on the handlebars, but then Frankie spots a squirrel and yanks her leash so hard he shouts and veers off the road, then flops over into a ditch. I race to see if he's hurt, but he's lying there laughing as Frankie licks his face.

"Told ya," I say.

"Yeah. You did." He laughs more, even though he's covered in grass stains and his shirt is wet. When he sits up, we find a small pocket of water under him, chock-full of tadpoles.

"There are so many," he says, poking his finger into the squirming mass.

Frankie lunges at the water but I hold her back. She does *not* need to eat tadpoles for dinner. "I think they're bullfrogs." A memory plays, of Dad showing me the tadpoles in the swampy part of our creek. "They lay their eggs in shallow water, but this will dry up soon."

Billy raises his dark eyebrows. "What should we do?"

"We need to get them to deeper water."

Really, there's only one place to take them.

Billy takes his shirt off to make a sling for the tad-poles, and there it is—a perfectly round birthmark on his pasty-white chest, exactly like the missing-child report said. It's weird to think I've really found Billy Holcomb. It doesn't feel good, knowing the truth while lying to everyone else, but maybe solving a mystery only feels good when you can share it with other people.

While we walk, I keep thinking about all the questions I want to ask him, but I'm not sure how to start. I don't even know if he wants to talk about what happened when he went missing.

Finally I blurt out, "The news said you were abducted. Is that true?"

"Yeah." His eyes are on the tadpoles. He shifts his grip on the T-shirt. "When I got to school, there was this car at the curb. The lady inside said my dad sent her to get me. I thought she was from his shop. She was wearing this big hat, but when I noticed she was going the wrong way, she took the hat off. It was Shailene. She looked different, but it was her."

"She kidnapped you! I knew it."

He shrugs. "She had this picture of us together, from before she went away. She said she came as soon as she could. I figured anything was better than staying with him."

"Aren't you mad at her for leaving, though?"

"She didn't go on purpose," he said quietly.

"Where was she?"

"She just couldn't come back, okay?"

"Okay."

We're quiet for a minute. The tadpoles squirm inside the shirt sling.

"My dad told me she didn't want to see me, but that was a lie," he says. "She wrote me letters. He tore them up, but sometimes I found them in the trash. It made him really mad when I did that. He got mad at me a lot after she was gone."

My blood runs cold. "What if he shows up again?"

"They'll arrest him."

I hope that's true.

We turn the corner and the Jessups' house comes into view. As soon as we step into their backyard, I spot Diesel throwing baseballs with Devin and Donny.

"Hurry," I tell Billy, and we shuffle to the pond with the tadpoles hanging between us. We scrape the tadpoles out of Billy's shirt as fast as we can, but Frankie starts barking and the Jessups see us. Diesel gets to the pond before we can leave.

"What are you doing?" he asks.

I give him the evil eye. "Why? You gonna tell me to scram?"

"No."

Devin and Donny can't believe it, either. "She's trespassing! Throw her out! Aw, D! Don't let her! She's got the poop touch!"

But no matter what they say, Diesel shakes his head.

Sometimes I do not understand people.

Billy tugs his wet shirt over his head, and we get out of there before Diesel changes his mind. At first I wonder if he feels sorry about being so mean to me now that we're helping Billy. Then something clicks and I realize Diesel wasn't running me off their property to be mean. He was protecting Billy and Shailene. I know it must be true, because it makes the most sense, and Stan says the simplest answer is usually the right one.

In the back of my head, I hear Cress telling me that I'm totally wrong about Diesel.

That's how she said it. *You're totally wrong about him.*

And for the first time, I wonder if maybe I am.

29

TALKING IN CODE

The fifth grade at my old elementary school celebrates the end of the year with a field trip to the amusement park. In my year, Lee Chen drank two slushies and threw up on the roller coaster. Sometimes I think I know exactly how he must have felt. Sick, overwhelmed, and powerless to stop it. I feel that way a lot, especially when I have to do something big.

Something that matters.

I'm supposed to use Mr. Hillman's visual organizer to plan my Living Museum essay, but the truth is, I haven't read much about Georgia O'Keeffe. It's not that I don't want to be her. She seems pretty cool. It's just that ever since I made that prop in art, this kernel of an idea has been lodged in my brain. I can feel it growing there, getting bigger every day.

I'm not sure what to do until library day, when we get to conference with Miss Rivera on our essays. I watch her go from table to table helping everyone with their problems, and I think maybe I should let her help me, too. I'm so used to never talking about Dad because it always turns into a Thing, but maybe this is when I'm *supposed* to talk about him.

Miss Rivera crosses to my table and plunks into a chair. She's wearing a shirt with a cat print and a fish pin that says *I Read Banned Books.* "Your turn to tell me something good, Maddy. I hope you've made some progress on your project?"

A storm gathers in my stomach, but I remind myself that Miss Rivera said we could propose our own historical figure if we could make a case for them.

"Miss Rivera?"

"Yes?"

She waits while I sit there, my stomach full of butterflies.

Finally I say, "Did you ever want to do something, but you weren't sure you could?"

Her eyes widen in surprise. "Well. Yes, actually."

She ducks her head a little. "I wanted to be an actress when I was younger. Very much. I still have moments of weakness when I think about what might've been." She laughs, but the sound is hollow.

"Why didn't you do it?"

"I guess I was scared." She gives a little sigh and smiles.

I'm scared, too. I don't know why it's so hard to say what I want. There are other kids waiting. I need to spit it out, but my mouth is so dry I can barely speak.

"Does our historical figure have to be someone important? Like, to lots of people?"

"Your figure can come from any walk of life," Miss Rivera says. "History is happening all around us. One day, the things we do may be written about in history books. What's important is that your figure brings new information to light. We study history so we can learn from the mistakes of the past, and from the successes. Everyone is important."

There's another long silence as I find the guts to ask my next question. I know Miss Rivera will be nice to me. I know she won't get *concerned*. But still, it's hard.

"Does my dad count?" I finally blurt out.

As I say the words, I feel like I'm falling, and not in a good way.

Miss Rivera places her hand on my arm. It feels light as a feather, and warm.

"Of course your father counts, Maddy," she says. "Of course he does."

Billy and I walk into the kitchen after school and find my mom teaching Shailene how to roll piecrust. Mom's wearing her apron and Shailene has a towel wrapped around her head, probably from another one of her long showers. There's flour everywhere, and I can see right away that her piecrust is too dry, but she's laughing that light laugh again, like she's a new person.

"What kind of pie are you making?" Billy asks.

"Lemon for you," Mom says. "And I was thinking about a chocolate mousse pie, too, seeing as it's so warm out." She looks at me. "Does that sound good?"

I have this weird urge to say *NO*, but I smile and agree anyway. I shouldn't be jealous of Shailene spending this time with Mom, but I still don't like what Shailene did. She kidnapped Billy, and it was scary, and I wish Mom remembered that.

They finish the pies while we do our homework.

Stan gets home at dinnertime and we eat a chicken pie that Mom and Shailene baked together. Billy keeps saying how delicious it is and moaning while he chews. It *is* really good, but when they ask my opinion, I say it's just okay.

"Soon you'll need two of these pies," Shailene says with a wink.

Mom goes still, and Stan's head snaps up.

"What does that mean?" I ask Mom.

A flush of warmth rushes through me.

"Mom, what does that *mean?*"

Shailene runs her hands over her face. "I'm so sorry. Me and my big mouth."

"It's okay," Mom says. She looks at me. "This wasn't how I planned on sharing this news, but I guess the cat's out of the bag." She looks at Stan. "I'm pregnant."

My heart clenches. I try not to feel crushed that she looked at him when she said it.

His eyes go wide, and then he breaks into a huge grin and jumps out of his chair to give Mom a hug. I know this is fine, and that I gave them my blessing, but I want to leave.

"Mads," Mom says, leaning close to me once Stan lets her go. "I'm so sorry it came out like this. It's still very, very early. I just found out myself, and I wasn't planning to say anything, but Shailene overheard my call with Dr. Udwadia's office."

"I'm really sorry," Shailene says. Her eyes say she means it, but I ignore her.

Mom presses a kiss to my cheek and I lean into her, breathing in her warm vanilla smell. "I love you so much, Maddy," she murmurs into my hair.

When I pull away, Stan tries to hug me, too, but I dodge him like I'm taking my plate to the sink and keep going until I'm out on the back deck. I flop onto a lounge chair and watch the dragonflies dart across the sky. After a minute, Billy flops into the chair next to me.

"Sorry about my mom," he says.

"So she's your mom now?" I snap, letting some of the nastiness spill right out.

He shrugs. "She tries to be. She's not good at this stuff."

"Like talking?"

He laughs. "Yeah. Like talking. She's no good at that." We're quiet for a while, and then he says, "Why do you hate your stepdad so much?"

"I don't *hate* him."

"Okay, but you don't *like* him."

"I do like him."

"You don't act like it."

Was that true? Did I treat Stan like dirt?

Billy tosses one of Frankie's tennis balls into the air. "He seems like a pretty nice guy."

"He *is* a nice guy," I repeat, and the words ring so true it hurts.

What kind of person takes someone else's kid to do fun stuff every weekend? Someone like Stan. I don't know what I'm holding out for. Dad isn't coming back. Ever.

I don't want to hang out with him. It's not like he's my real dad or anything!

That's what Stan heard me say when Mom brought up the whole idea of me and Stan spending time together. He acted like he hadn't heard it, but his face was pink, so I knew he did. And the worst part was that I didn't even mean it, not the way it sounded.

I didn't hate Stan. I just didn't want to lose Dad.

Lying there next to Billy, listening to the tree frogs chirping in the trees, I start thinking that maybe the first step to getting rid of that barrier is fixing things with Stan.

After a while, Stan joins us on the deck. He has his little red notebook as usual.

"Did you know you can talk in binary code?" he asks.

This is such a Stan thing that I almost laugh.

"Like computers?" Billy says.

"Yes. Exactly like computers. Each letter in the alphabet has a number, and that number can be made from an eight-digit sequence of zeroes and ones. Each place has a value starting with one and doubling with each place. For example, the letter A is equal to the number 65, which is 01000001 in binary. So if I say 01001000 01001001, that means 'Hi.' Neat, huh?"

Billy's mouth hangs open. "That is *so cool*," he says.

Stan looks at me with hope in his eyes.

I smile. "It's very cool."

That night, after I snuggle up to Croc and tell Dad about my day, I spend some time looking up how to say things in binary, only a few letters. Then I give Dad's picture a kiss and text him, "010000100 01111001 01100101." It's not good-bye forever. Just for the night.

30

MIRACLE MUD

Next to our house, Cress's house is my favorite place to hang out. There are Bollywood posters and decorations from Carnival, and the kitchen always smells like a delicious blend of coconut and spice. They keep snow cones in the freezer, but her dad will put hot sauce on your pizza if you aren't looking. When we walk in, he's shouting at a soccer match on the TV, so we go straight to Cress's room, where she has a box of mud masks waiting on her bed.

"Miracle Mud," I read off the box as she grabs some washcloths.

"It's amazing," she says. "You can feel it pulling your skin tight."

"Why would I want to pull my skin tight?"

She makes a face. "It cleans your skin. I did one with Mia and my cousins, and all this gunk came out of my pores! It's there, you just can't see it."

I look at my face in her mirror. Do I even have pores?

Meanwhile, Cress grabs a bowl of warm water and gel pads that look like superhero masks for our eyes. She lays everything on her desk in a neat row.

"First we have to wash with warm water," she says. "It's important to relax the skin and open the pores before you do the mask." She hands me a washcloth and dips hers into the bowl of warm water, wringing it out carefully before pressing the wet cloth to her face.

I do the same thing and stand there with the hot washcloth over my eyes, feeling silly. It *is* nice and warm, though, and breathing against the fabric makes me sound like Darth Vader.

"How long do we stand here?"

"Two minutes," Cress says.

I breathe louder against the fabric. "You underestimate the power of the Dark Side."

She giggles. "You are so weird."

"You're the one making me do this!"

She thumps my arm, and I try to thump her back, but she dodges me. Once our washcloths have cooled, we use the sticks that came in the box to apply the mask. The mud is slimy and black, like tar, and it sticks to *everything*. Soon I have it on my clothes and in my hair.

Cress tries to wipe the mud out of my hair. "Seriously, Mads? It's not *that* hard."

"Well, I've never done it before."

"Whose fault is that?" Cress says, which stings a little. Normally I don't mind joking about how much I hate this kind of stuff, but I don't like that Cress is so into it now. Her room has changed, too. The turtle pictures that were around her mirror at our last sleepover are gone. In their place are long strips of photo-booth pictures with Cress and Mia and their cousins.

"You have to get used to it," Cress says.

I'm not sure I want to get used to it.

"Did you bring the clue notebook?" she asks. "Maybe my mom can help us."

My face flushes under my mask. "I forgot it. Sorry."

Cress frowns, but she doesn't say anything else.

When the timer on her phone buzzes, it's time to peel our masks off. The mud has dried into grayish-blackish plastic. Cress rubs at the edge of her mask and starts peeling it off like a layer of Saran Wrap. I try to do the same thing, but it feels like I'm ripping my skin off.

"Ow! Ow, ow, ow!"

"What's wrong?" Cress says, coming closer.

"It hurts so much! Am I bleeding?" I half expect to see red on my fingertips.

She makes a face. "It's not that bad."

"Bald spot! Broken dishwasher!" I curse, hopping around like I can somehow get away from the pain if I keep moving. "This doesn't hurt you?"

"Seriously, Mads. Calm down. You probably have more hair on your face than me."

I freeze. Hair. *On my face?*

A sick feeling gathers in the pit of my stomach.

I don't like the way Cress is looking at me, like I'm such a wimp when this hurts enough to make my eyes water. "Just help me get it off," I say, trying not to cry.

Eventually, we pull the mask free, but my face is red and blotchy. Cress's skin is a smooth, even brown. She doesn't even look sorry. She frowns like she's mad at me.

"I guess I'm not very good at mud masks," I say. "Sorry."

She bites her lip. "I'm trying to help you be a little more normal."

My face gets even hotter. "You're the one who's doing weird stuff."

"Excuse me?"

"Like, wearing makeup and your whole new look and flirting with Diesel Jessup!"

Her eyes go wide. "That doesn't make me weird. I like Mia's makeup tricks. I like my hair, too. I'm tired of little-kid poufs. And you're the one with the boyfriend. I see Eric getting on and off at your stop. I'm not clueless, you know. You could have told me."

I stare at her, and all I can think is, *What happened to my best friend?* Because this is not her. "What is *up* with you?" I finally say.

"Me?" She shakes her head and turns away to clean up the mess from the mud masks.

I want to do something that will snap us back to reality, where she is a genius and I am awkward, but we get along like peanut butter and jelly. Only I don't know how to do that.

The rest of the sleepover is the same as it always is. Cress's dad cooks stewed chicken and rice for dinner. After her mom gets home, we play board games together. Mia is out with her friends, and I'm glad, because maybe that means Cress and I can get back to normal.

I want everything to go back to the way it used to be.

All night, I try to crack jokes, but Cress doesn't laugh. I want to tell her about everything that's going on, about Mom having a baby and what I'm planning to do for my

Living Museum project, even the truth about Billy and Shailene, but it feels like a barrier is growing between us now, cutting us off from each other the way the Miracle Mud sealed our skin from the air.

When we lie down to sleep that night, for the first time ever, that's exactly what we do.

We just go straight to sleep.

31

THE PLAN

I get back from Cress's house earlier than I've ever gotten back before. I'm kind of looking forward to hanging out with Stan, but it turns out he has to go to work for a big code conversion, so we won't get to visit the Arboretum. I should be thrilled, but instead I kind of miss our goofy trip. I guess any routine can become something you count on over time.

After Stan leaves, Mom and Shailene huddle in the dining room, sorting through the huge pile of papers. "Once we get all of this organized, we'll see what Renée has to say. She must know someone who's willing to work pro bono." Mom looks at me. "Can I help you?"

"You mean Renée, Cress's mom?"

"Yes," Mom says. "She's going to connect Shailene

with a family lawyer who can represent her if she needs to go back to court."

"*If* I can afford it," Shailene says. There are bundles of cash on the table, but I'm still stuck on the part where Mom has told Cress's mom about Shailene and Billy.

"If you told Cress's mom, why can't I tell Cress?"

"Because Renée is an adult. She isn't going to say anything that could cause problems."

I cross my arms. "Just because we're kids doesn't mean we'll mess up."

Mom sighs. "I know that, honey. I need you to trust me on this."

But I don't. Part of me still thinks we should call Sheriff Dobbs and let him handle all of this. I'm not even convinced that we should be helping Shailene.

"You know she tricked him? She told Billy she worked for his dad. She *kidnapped* him."

Mom's mouth opens in horror. "Maddy!"

"No, it's okay," Shailene says. "I'd think the same thing if I was her." She looks at me, but for once she's not staring bloody murder. "Look, I haven't always made the best choices. I know that. I'm sorry for taking him like that. I couldn't leave him there another day."

"Maybe you shouldn't have left him there in the first place."

Shailene's jaw goes tight, but she doesn't say a word.

"What's done is done," Mom says, giving me a pointed look. "Let's stay focused on finding you a new place. I spoke with my friend at the Domestic Violence Center. She said to check with the Battered Women's Ministry to see if they have any low-income housing options."

Shailene says, "I can handle it," but those words echo in my head.

Domestic violence. Battered women.

"I saw those scars on Billy's arm," I say, and Mom inhales sharply.

Shailene rubs a hand over her face. "I got married before I really knew Billy's dad," she says. "We had a baby, and I thought things might get better. Then I broke a plate and he broke my jaw." She gives a small, sad laugh. "I knew he'd go after Billy once I was gone. I felt sick every single day, knowing he was there with that man. I'll never forgive myself for that."

My heart hurts, hearing all this, but before I can speak the doorbell rings.

We all jump half out of our skins.

A split second later, Billy barges into the kitchen from the garage, where Frankie is barking her head off. "It's the police," he says. "The police are here."

There are moments when time seems to slow down. It's like I'm inside a bubble where the sounds are muffled and the outside world is blurry. The only thing I can hear is the *crash, crash, crash* of the waves and my own heart beating like it's trying to take flight. In these moments, it's hard to move, the same way that it's hard to move in a nightmare.

"Stay calm," Mom says in her nurse's voice, the one she uses when I'm bleeding or barfing. "Go sit down while I see what they want. Everything is going to be okay."

I look at Billy. He's clinging to his mother's arm like a possum to a branch.

My fingers twitch, and my toes. I can move again. "Come on," I say, and they follow me into the living room. Billy tucks in next to Shailene on the couch.

"I got you," she says, her arm wrapping around him. "I got you."

She did a bad thing, kidnapping him, but right now she looks like she would do anything to protect him. I used to think I knew what was bad or good, but now I'm not so sure. Maybe we're never just good or just bad. Maybe we're always a mix of both.

The front door opens, and we hear Mom's voice and

two others—a man and a woman—and then Mom's walking into the living room with two uniformed officers behind her.

Billy's eyes go wide and white.

"Good afternoon, ma'am," the woman officer says. "We're sorry to disturb you, but we need to inform you that your husband, Robert Holcomb, was arrested in Fayetteville early yesterday morning for violating your court order of protection."

My heart ricochets in my chest. Mr. Holcomb was *arrested.*

I look at Billy, but he's staring at the floor like he wants to disappear.

"You should also be aware that as of this morning, Mr. Holcomb has made bail and has been released pending a hearing on the court order violation."

Billy's eyes snap up. "You let him out?"

The male officer steps in. "Mr. Holcomb paid the assigned bail and was released this morning. If you hear from him again or if he comes within two hundred feet of you, he will be arrested and charged with further violation of the protection order."

Shailene glares at the officer. "That didn't stop him the first time."

The female officer sighs in sympathy. "Well, hopefully

he'll think differently now that he's spent a night behind bars."

"There must be something else we can do," Mom says.

The male officer frowns. "If you see him again, call us."

They turn to leave, and Mom sees them out. A minute later, their car crunches along our gravel driveway. When Frankie stops barking, we know they're gone.

Mom comes back into the living room with a plate of cookies, but there are shiny tracks on her cheeks, and her eyes have that too-bright sheen of tears.

"We should go," Shailene says. "I have friends in San Francisco. We can go there."

Mom shakes her head, but inside I'm wondering if maybe they should leave.

If Mr. Holcomb thinks they're in the area, he could come *here* looking for them.

"I don't want to go to California," Billy says.

His voice trembles, and inside my chest, so does my heart.

Mom raises her hands. "Let's all catch our breath, okay? No one has to go anywhere right this minute." She looks at me, and I know what she's thinking. We're not letting them leave. We're not losing anyone else.

"Are you sure about this?" Shailene asks.

It's scary to think that Mr. Holcomb could be out there right now, looking for us, but if they leave, they'll be on their own. They may not be family, but they are our friends.

I nod at Mom.

"Yes," she says. "We're sure. We're sticking to the plan."

32

A DIFFERENT WORLD

"**S**he's not as mean as she seems, is she?" I look at Billy as he brushes the dryer vent clean. We're doing safety checks while the grown-ups talk on the back deck. Shailene is smoking a cigarette, which Mom would normally flip about, but I guess there are exceptions to everything.

"Who?" Billy says.

"Your mom."

He shrugs. "She's used to people giving her a hard time."

"Why?"

He finishes with the dryer vent and hands me the brush. Then he looks at me for a long time, long enough for my face to start going hot. The blue has faded from his hair. I can see the dark roots that match his dark eyebrows. "She was in jail."

"What?"

"That's where she was, when she was gone. She was in jail." He looks at my list like he hasn't just blown my mind. "What's next?"

We move on to trimming the bushes.

I want to ask what Shailene went to jail for, but it feels too much like the bad kind of prying I heard so much after Dad died.

"You were right about my dad," I blurt out. "He drowned." I don't know why, but my heart is racing. I think maybe I'm bracing for Billy to give me that look. The pity one.

But he doesn't.

He gives me this serious nod and goes back to trimming the bushes.

I think of how hard Billy worked to protect that trailer with his traps, and how gentle he is with Frankie, and how his face lights up at the sight of a pie, and it's impossible to imagine a father who would hurt him. I think about how his father might be out there right now and wish we had a motion-sensor alarm. I think of the little person growing in Mom's belly, and how I know Stan will be a good dad. When the baby cries, he'll hold her in his arms and rock her to sleep. I think back to the beginning of the school year, when Mom and Stan had just gotten married, and my biggest struggle was figuring out how to hang out with him.

It feels like a very long time ago. It feels like a whole different world.

We go about our lives like everything is normal. We play board games. We have Sunday dinner. We wake up Monday morning and get ready for school. Stan offers to drive us, but I want to talk to Cress. She hasn't answered any of my texts since I slept over at her house, and I know she has phone privileges.

This time, when I climb the bus steps with Billy, Cress isn't in our seat. She's in the back with Diesel. She must know I'm there, but she won't meet my eyes.

I drop into our seat and pretend to work on my Living Museum packet. I brought it to show to Cress, but she's not there to give me a thumbs-up.

This time, the answers are up to me.

When I walk into the library, Miss Rivera gives me a little wave. She's wearing a shirt that says *Never Argue with a Librarian. They Know Too Much!* There are five minutes until the bell rings.

That's long enough to look something up, if I want to.

That tipping feeling pulls at me again, but I remind myself that I was the one who found Billy Holcomb. Cress helped me with the binder, but I was the one who did it. If I can do that, then I can do this.

"Here goes nothing," I text Dad.

I take a deep breath and put my fingers on the keyboard.

I search the name *Todd Gaines*.

And I begin to read.

33

THE FACTS

The day my father died, it was eighty-two degrees at the beach.

The date was June 2.

The wind was blowing from the southeast at nine miles per hour.

High tide occurred between two and three o'clock.

We did not notice the red flags on the lifeguard's station.

We weren't worried that the station was empty.

We could not see the rip current in the water.

34

CODE YELLOW

When we get home from school in the afternoon, Shailene's pacing in the kitchen, twisting her hands something fierce. "It was his car," she says. "I know it."

"What model was it again?" Mom asks.

"A midnight-blue Mustang. Right out there in your court."

Mom jots something down on the little pad of paper she keeps by the phone.

"I should've known better," Shailene says. "Why did I file that police report?"

In some emergency warning systems, color-coding is used to indicate how bad the threat is. Green means things are normal and there's nothing to worry about.

Red means you're in huge trouble. And code yellow means trouble is on the horizon.

This is a code yellow at least.

"What is it?" I ask Mom. "What happened?"

"Is it Dad?" Billy says. "Did he find us?"

"I'm so sorry, honey," Shailene says, her voice tight. "I think he did."

That's when we go to code red.

Shailene tries to hug Billy, but he dodges her and goes into the living room.

Mom hugs her instead. "It's okay. It's going to be okay." She looks at me over Shailene's shoulder, and I know she's saying it to me, too. Every fiber of my being wants to call Sheriff Dobbs right that second, but I force myself to walk into the living room, where Billy is crouched on the floor, hacking at a stick with a Swiss Army knife over an old towel.

This one time after Dad died, there was a grocery clerk at the Food Lion who recognized me from the news. She had big hair and red lips. When she looked at me, her face all excited, I felt like I had three heads. I wanted to disappear, the way Billy is trying to disappear now.

I crouch next to him. "What're you making?"

"Spike balls. You hang them in the trees. When

someone trips the trigger, bam." He holds up a clump of spikes tied together with twine and lets it drop. The spikes stab the air.

"Good idea." I unroll a loop of twine and join him.

When Stan gets home, Mom is quick to fill him in. Shailene is finally calm enough to sit on the couch and watch a movie with Billy, who has worn himself out carving wood spikes.

I try to imagine what it's like to need booby traps to protect yourself from your own father, but I can't. Fathers are supposed to protect *you*. They're bigger, stronger, and tougher—all so they can keep you alive. Even if it costs them everything.

Stan leaves to meet Mr. Jessup, and I follow him into the garage. Frankie pops up from her bed. I drop down and hug her side, like that's the reason I'm out there in the first place.

"What are you gonna do?" I ask Stan.

"We'll start at the top of the subdivision and work our way back. We'll have to check each street individually. Still, it shouldn't take too long."

I nod like I'm approving his plan, when really I'm wondering what will happen if they find Mr. Holcomb

out there in his midnight-blue Mustang. Stan's not exactly a tough guy.

Frankie licks my face. "What if you find him?"

"I don't think we will," Stan says matter-of-factly. "If he wanted to confront us, he would have done it already. I doubt he would stick around and risk being discovered."

"Why does he keep coming after them?"

"I imagine he thinks that if he finds them, he'll get his way."

I think of the scars on Billy's arm. "He's a bully."

Stan stops and looks at me. "Sometimes when people are hurting, they lash out. They might have addiction or anger issues. What grown-ups do doesn't always make sense."

"Like hurting your own kid?"

He nods. "Abuse isn't about love. It's about control. And it's wrong."

I know that. But I also know it's wrong for Mr. Holcomb to be out there, free as a bird.

"What did Shailene go to jail for?"

He considers me for a second. "Drugs. She has an addiction, which isn't a choice. It's an illness. My father struggled with alcohol addiction his whole life. He passed away from liver disease when I was twenty-six."

"Wait, your dad died?"

Stan nods. "He did."

A shock wave passes through me, and it's like I'm seeing Stan in a whole new light. Same glasses, same skinny frame, but we have this one huge thing in common.

How didn't I know this about him?

Then I remember that I haven't really asked Stan these kinds of questions. We talk, but I don't know much about his life before us. And he doesn't know much about my life before him.

"I'm sorry," I say.

He smiles. "It's okay. He stopped drinking for a while, but in the end he couldn't quit. It's hard not to be mad at him, but it helps to remember all the good things he did. He took me to museums. He got me my first computer. He wasn't a bad person, he made bad choices. Shailene got clean, got her GED, and did rehab. She's turned her life around."

I think of the sign in the Jessups' trailer. *Life Is a Work in Progress.*

"There's no such thing as good guys and bad guys," Stan says. "There are just people. We can save a life on Monday and take a life on Tuesday. It all depends on what we do on any given day. I like to believe that every human being has a chance at redemption."

"Even Mr. Holcomb?"

"I hope so."

I wish I could be as hopeful as Stan, but I don't think there's a lick of good in Mr. Holcomb. Stan finishes getting the car ready while I pet Frankie, who slowly melts to the floor and rolls over into her favorite position, upside down with her paws hanging in the air. She doesn't even have to think about loving. It's what she does.

Stan climbs into the car and my heart squeezes tight. What am I afraid of, anyway? If I try and we don't click, the world won't end. We will still be here.

Before he shuts the door, I call out, "Hey, Stan!"

He looks at me, his brows raised.

"Be careful, okay?"

35

PLAYING PRETEND

S tan and Mr. Jessup don't find any sign of Mr.
Holcomb, but Shailene still says Billy needs to stay
home from school. They have lots of packing to do,
anyway, now that she's signed a lease on a new place. I
have to go to school, but I ask Stan to drive me instead
of riding the bus. It hurts too much to see Cress sitting
with Diesel.

I know I should forget my promise to Mom and
tell Cress what's going on, but I can't get over the fact
that she would ditch me for Diesel Jessup. A real friend
wouldn't do that, no matter how weird I was acting. At
least that's what I tell myself.

At school, I keep my eyes on the floor and ignore
everyone around me. If I don't see Cress, I can pretend

she doesn't exist. She can't hurt me if she doesn't exist.

My strategy works until art class on Thursday.

Everyone's finishing their models for the Living Museum. My site level is nearly complete. I've added three coats of newspaper and painted it bright yellow with orange lettering and black trim. After I carefully glue a circle of plastic to the end as a lens, it's finished.

When I set my model on the rack to dry, I see that kids have made all kinds of things, like an old-fashioned camera, an Olympic torch, a big curly beard out of shredded paper, and even a full-size voting booth. I keep looking until I find Cress's *Friendship 7* model. It's in the very back, and it's kind of a mess. I can see what she was trying to do, but the papier-mâché is too floppy to make the steel legs that prop up the bottom of the capsule. She needs to use straws to make the legs stiffer and hold the body of the model off the table.

It makes it worse, knowing she needs me and I'm letting her down. Just because you can't see someone doesn't mean you won't miss them. I should know. I'm the one who talks to Dad's photo every night and texts him all the time, half hoping he'll text me back one day.

Before I leave, I put a few straws next to Cress's model where she's sure to find them.

Billy's been quiet in the days since Shailene saw Mr. Holcomb's car, but when I get home there's a strange light in his eyes. "Let's go for a bike ride," he says.

"No," Shailene says. "No going outside."

Billy braces his arms on the kitchen doorframe and starts climbing. His bare toes grip the edges of the molding like a frog, propelling him upward in goofy, scrambling hops.

Shailene jumps to her feet, looking like she's about to go grab him. "What on earth are you doing? Get down before you ruin the walls!"

He drops to the floor with a thud. "Let me go outside!" His eyes gleam with something dangerous that needs to break free.

"I'll go with him," I say. "We won't go near the road."

After a long, tense moment, Shailene finally agrees. We can go outside, but we can't ride around the neighborhood. Which is fine. There are plenty of things to do in the woods.

Frankie gallops ahead as we run across Dad's field and down the slope to the gully, where the creek washes up quartz and arrowheads in silty drifts. Billy charges down the steep clay bank with his arms pinwheeling. I

hop down after him, trying not to scratch my arms. Now that we're further into April, the briars have come back to life. They're thick along the edges of the gully, but thin out toward the water. Dad said briars don't love getting their roots wet. That little bit of open space has let a few thin saplings take root.

Billy fishes a branch out of the water and whacks one of the skinny saplings so hard the trunk vibrates. His stick makes a weird kind of music, like a drumbeat.

Whack, whack, whack!

I grab a stick and join in, smacking another tree until my stick breaks. Billy's stick breaks, too, but he keeps hitting and hitting that tree. *Whack, whack, whack!*

He's not smiling anymore.

"Billy," I say, but he keeps whaling on that tree. His hands are red with effort. There are tears in his eyes. "Billy, stop." He ignores me. The wildness has taken over.

"I hate him!" he shouts. "I *hate* him!"

"Billy!"

"I. Don't. Want. To. GO!" He smacks the trunk as hard as he can with each word. Then he stops and stands there panting, his arms hanging limp.

"Where're you going?" a voice says from overhead.

We look up at the edge of the gully and find Diesel Jessup staring down at us.

Frankie seems to have run off somewhere, probably chasing squirrels. I put my hands on my hips and give Diesel my meanest face. "What're you doing here?"

"Me first." He looks at Billy. "Where are you going?"

"We're moving," Billy says.

"When?"

"It's none of your business," I say. "You shouldn't even *be* here."

Diesel's nostrils flare. "Oh, come on. Enough with the territory wars."

"*Enough?* You're the one who stole my bike! You said you'd rip my arms off!"

"I thought it was a game!" he shouts back.

Which is like a bucket of water dumped over my flames.

"I didn't take your bike," he says. "My little brothers did that." He rubs the back of his neck. "I didn't know they were gonna do it or I would've stopped them."

Billy laughs. "Devin and Donny took her bike?"

"Yeah," Diesel says. "I don't even like Kool-Aid Jammers."

My head spins while I try to wrap my brain around this new information. Diesel didn't take my bike? The territory wars were just a game? "But you were going to smash my tire."

He laughs. "Come on. I was kidding, Gaines."

"You were not!"

He puts his hands up. "Okay, maybe I was a little serious, but it was a dare game, right? You say this and I say that and we go back and forth until one of us gives."

Really? Was it *me* who'd been fighting Diesel all this time? I think back to what he said when he warned me to stay away from Billy.

"What about when you called me a freak?"

Diesel's smile vanishes. "I'm sorry I said that. My daddy told me to make sure no one went back by the trailer, and I got caught up in doing the job. I was wrong."

Apologies must be contagious, because as soon as I hear him say that I say, "I'm sorry I threw dog poop at you."

Billy's mouth falls open. "You threw *dog poop* at him?"

"It was in a *bag*."

"It's fine," Diesel says. "We're good."

There is a long moment of silence while me and Billy and Diesel all look at each other, trying to make sense of what just happened here. Did Diesel and I just become friends again?

"Sorry I got on your case," he says to Billy. "We've been worried about y'all since you moved over here. Dad's a mess."

Billy's face falls. "I'm tired of moving, but if my dad finds us, we're dead."

I put my hand on his shoulder.

"You can come live with us," Diesel says. "My dad'll fix it."

"I'll help, too," I say, wishing there was something more I could do.

Frankie finally comes running back into the gully. She doesn't even bark at Diesel when she sees him. "Some watchdog you are," I say. She starts licking Billy's hands and legs, any part of him she can reach until he finally cracks a smile.

"Don't you have some booby traps that need setting?" I ask.

Billy gives me a funny look. "I'm not supposed to go out front."

"I won't tell," Diesel says.

I nod. "Me neither."

Billy grins. "Let's do it."

36

RUNNING THE GAUNTLET

I have to do something about me and Cress. As I climb onto the bus Friday morning, I know this, but my heart thumps as I walk up the steps. I feel like I'm stepping directly into the open during a game of hide-and-seek. Cress has no reason to forgive me, but I'm ready to apologize. I should have listened to her when she tried to tell me about Diesel.

My stomach dips as I walk toward the back of the bus. The aisle is a dangerous path filled with knees and elbows and book bags. It's like running the gauntlet. And if you don't get where you're going quickly, the floor lurches beneath your feet and sends you tumbling.

There are two empty seats about halfway down.

And then there's Cress. She's in the back with Diesel

again, only this morning when he sees me coming he gives me this tiny nod, like he's telling me I can do this.

My feet scramble over people and book bags until I reach the back of the bus.

Cress looks up at me. "What do you want?" she asks.

I want to say I'm sorry. I want to tell her the truth about Billy. I want to be friends again.

"Did you see the straws I left you?" I ask.

"What?"

Diesel slides his hand across his neck in warning, but Cress is waiting for an answer.

"The straws for your *Friendship 7* model? I left some on the art rack for you. They should help make the legs stronger, so it can stand up. The papier-mâché is too soft on its own."

I smile, but Cress's eyes narrow.

"You're the one who squished my model?" she says. "*You?*"

"What? No! I didn't—someone squished your model?"

Cress looks away from me, her jaw clenched.

I am the world's worst apologizer. Diesel makes this jerking motion with his big block head, like I should leave, but I'm not going to walk away when Cress is upset.

The bus driver shouts at me to sit down *NOW*, so I cram into the seat across from them. The kid sitting there complains as I squish him with my book bag, but he'll live.

"Cress," I say. *"Cress."*

She finally looks at me. "Where's your new best friend?" she says.

"Who?"

"Eric. You know, the one you *ditched me for?"*

"He's sick," I lie, because that's what Mom told me to say if anyone asked. I'd rather tell Cress the truth, but I can't do it here. Not on the bus. Not in front of Diesel.

"Can we talk?" I ask her.

She crosses her arms. "I shouldn't have to explain why my hair looks different, or why I changed my clothes. You're supposed to be my *friend.*"

"You're right," I say, and she sits back a little. Her eyes shine with tears.

I was wrong. Cress hasn't stepped into her new self, but she's trying to. Just like I'm trying to. And she needs her friend. Just like I do.

"Why are you acting so weird?" she says. "You're obsessed with this new kid, then he's getting on the bus with you every morning and you won't tell me what's going on. We're supposed to have a blood oath."

"You guys took a blood oath?" Diesel says. "That's so cool."

I ignore him. "I know. I'm sorry. I can explain—"

Diesel shoots me a warning look.

"—but I can't do it here. Can we talk? After school?"

Cress bites her lip. "I don't know. I have ballet."

"Since when do you take ballet?"

"Since I got back from Atlanta. You've been too busy to notice."

She's right. I have been busy, and I haven't been there for my friend. She was trying to help me, and I shut her out. "You were right about him," I say, nodding at Diesel. "He didn't take my bike. I'm sorry I didn't listen to you before."

"To be fair, we were in a war," Diesel says. "I mean, it was only a game, but she didn't know it. It's okay. My little brothers get confused, too."

I slap his arm. "I wasn't *confused*."

"Just sayin'!" he says as Cress watches us, surprised.

The bus swings onto the road that leads to the middle school.

"Can I call you this weekend?" I ask Cress.

She doesn't say anything for a minute.

"I think she's really sorry," Diesel says. "I mean, she sure looks like she is."

Cress's mouth stretches into a smile in spite of itself, revealing the gleam of her braces.

"Maybe," she says.

And that is good enough for me.

37

GREAT MINDS

ttics are strange places. Today when I pull the hatch in the upstairs hallway, dust swirls through the opening. Usually, Mom's the only one who comes up here, when it's time for holiday decorations or when I've outgrown my clothes and she puts them away for donation. Now I'm the one on the hunt, this time for Dad's stuff to use in the Living Museum.

The folding stairs wobble as I climb up. The air is warm and dusty, but in a good way, like quilts and books. Overhead, the roof narrows to a sharp ridge, as if I'm inside the hull of a ship, only upside down. Thick, roughhewn boards line the floor. Boxes line the eaves. Mom has labeled most of them. *Christmas. Easter. Baby Clothes. Donation.*

I poke along the edges, peering behind the boxes into the steep, slanted space where the roof meets the walls of the house. Behind the *Christmas Lights* box is a faded green canvas bag.

My heart skips a beat.

It's not easy to squeeze behind the Christmas boxes, but I duck my head and try not to step off the rafters into the insulation, where Dad once warned my foot could go through the ceiling. I remember thinking that if I did fall through, I'd land somewhere else, maybe a place full of fairies and ponies. Now I know it's just my bedroom beneath this part of the attic.

After I drag the canvas bag free, I settle on the attic floor to open it.

My chest squeezes like it's in a vise. I'm not sure what I'm going to find inside this dusty old thing. Probably nothing other than Dad's old surveyor's tripod, but it still feels like I'm about to fall through the ceiling and land somewhere new.

Outside, car tires crunch down our gravel driveway.

I pull out my phone and text, "I found your stuff, Dad."

Then, before I lose my nerve, I pull the thick copper zipper down the length of the canvas bag, revealing a folded tripod and a dozen clear plastic tubes with rolled-up papers in them.

I was expecting the tripod, but the tubes are a surprise. This is how Dad stored his survey papers so they would be safe from water and bugs. I pull one of the tubes from the bag and spin it, looking for the label, but the outside is unmarked. The cap twists off after a couple of tries and the rolled-up paper slides into my hand. It's not easy to lay it flat after all these years, but when I finally manage to pin down the corners with some boxes, I find a detailed drawing of our property.

I run my fingers over the paper's smooth surface.

There are so many familiar details, like the gully and the rock at the top of our driveway. The creek is drawn in dashes. Arrows extend from many of the lines, marking the coordinates with neat rows of numbers. The box in the bottom corner says *Green Thumb Land Surveyors,* which was Dad's survey company, but the project name is *Gaines Property Extension.*

Inside another tube is a drawing of our house, but where the deck is now, the drawing shows a whole new section of house. The bottom floor is labeled as a sunroom and the top floor is labeled as a third bedroom. Lightly penciled letters in Dad's handwriting spell out *Nursery.* My heart lurches.

Dad was planning to expand the house.

He was planning to have another *kid.*

It's always felt so wrong to go on without him, but maybe that's not what we're doing. Dad's life was interrupted, like mine and Mom's, but none of us planned on that. He expected to go on. Maybe I should, too.

Feet creak on the stairs, and I wipe the tears off my face so Mom won't think I'm upset, but it's Stan who appears in the opening.

He sees me and jumps a little. "Hey, kiddo. I didn't realize you were up here." He has a brown paper shopping bag that he's trying to hide behind his back.

"I was looking for something."

I slide the boxes off the corners of Dad's papers and they spring back into rolls.

Stan hesitates, uncertain if he should come up or not.

"Whatever you're hiding up here, I won't tell," I say as I slide the papers back inside their tubes, which is hard to do without creasing them.

"I don't want to intrude," Stan says, still uncertain.

"It's okay. I was getting some of Dad's stuff for my Living Museum project."

Stan finally comes closer. The shopping bag has an oval stamp on it with the store name: *Little Wonders.* "Did you find everything you need?" he asks.

"Yeah." My fingers hesitate. Then I tip the drawing of our house out of the tube again and spread it out so Stan

can see it. He sets his bag down and crouches next to me.

"Oh, wow. This is the house." His fingers travel over the kitchen and the den. I can tell when he sees Dad's note about the nursery because his hand stops moving.

"I guess Dad was thinking the same thing as you and Mom," I say, wondering how Stan will take it. I would probably be jealous, but he smiles.

"Great minds think alike," he says.

Then he reaches inside the shopping bag and lifts out a blue box covered in yellow stars.

"I was going to wait to try this out until your mom wasn't around, but she won't catch us up here," he says as he opens the box and pulls out a small white dome with a cord.

There are no power outlets up here, but there is an extension cord in the corner, which I unwind while Stan pops down the stairs to plug it in.

When he gets back, he turns the attic light off and connects the dome to the cord.

Stars fill the room, turning the tiny attic into an endless galaxy.

I gasp as they rotate slowly around us.

"'For small creatures such as we, the vastness is bearable only through love,'" Stan says with a smile. "Carl Sagan said that. He was a fellow star nerd. You'd like him." He watches for a minute, his face reflecting the stars. "They say the shapes and movement are soothing for infants, but your mom probably knows better than me. Do you think she'll like it?"

The stars wink a little, on and off, like they are coming to life.

"She won't like it," I say. "She'll love it."

38

A PERSON-SHAPED LUMP

Sometimes, after I talk to Dad's photo and curl up with Croc to fall asleep, I dream about Dad. Usually I can't see his face, but I know it's him by the way he feels: steady, warm, and strong. He's both Dad and Not Dad, and sometimes he morphs into other people— Grandma Evans, Miss Rivera, or even my math teacher— but never Stan.

My brain keeps them separate, like there is a barrier in my dreams, too.

The night that Stan shows me the star machine, suddenly they are both there. Dad, strong and steady. Stan, fading in and out of Dad's image like an old-timey movie reel.

I try to say something to them, but my mouth isn't

working. My lips are stuck together, and no matter how hard I try to speak, the words won't come. I try harder.

My eyelids flutter.

I start to realize that I'm dreaming and none of this is real, but for a few seconds, I see Dad and Stan so clearly in my mind that I bolt upright, looking for them across the room.

What I find is Billy, standing at my window, staring outside.

"Fudgesicle! What on earth are you doing in here?"

Billy holds a finger to his lips and motions for me to come over.

I tug on my socks and slip out of bed, hugging my pajamas to my sides. When I get to the window, I look outside but don't see anything. Not at first.

He points at something. "By the crooked tree. Next to the driveway."

My eyes seek the outline of the tree that died over the winter. Most of its branches have already fallen off and the trunk leans a little to one side, like a person about to fall over. The moon is covered, the clouds low and gray, so it takes me a while to figure out where the edge of the tree turns into the edge of the driveway, but when I do, my breath catches.

There is a person-shaped lump leaning against the tree.

As we watch, a lighter flares. The shadow person's face glows to life for a second, then disappears, leaving only a tiny orange circle of light—a lit cigarette.

I scramble back from the window, afraid of being spotted.

"Do you see him, too?" Billy asks. "I thought maybe I was imagining it."

"Yes, I see him." My heart pounds against my ribs. "You think that's your dad?"

Billy nods slowly, his mouth a grim line.

"Aren't you scared?"

"No." He huffs like I called him a baby. "I'm not scared of him."

"I didn't mean it like that. Look, there's scary, and there's crud-your-pants scary. This is crud-your-pants scary." Something clicks. "We should get Stan."

Billy clenches his fists. "I'll show him who's scary." He turns away from the window like he's planning to charge outside all by himself.

I grab at his arm. "Hold on! Just wait a second!" Then it comes to me—what Cress said before. "We need a picture. Evidence."

Billy hesitates, and I hurry to my bedside table, feeling around in the dark for my phone.

"We should've put the traps by the driveway," he says.

"We can later."

"I'm sick of this," he says. "I'm sick of always hiding."

Finally, my fingers hit hard plastic. I grab my phone and run to the window, but my camera won't focus on the shadows outside. "Come *on*," I say, trying another angle.

Billy comes back to the window and leans over my shoulder.

The clouds shift overhead, revealing the glow of a half-full moon. As moonlight trickles through the leaves, the woods brighten, transforming into a tangle of dark lines against a blue-white background. Somewhere in the distance, a car backfires.

Billy frowns. "He's gone."

I hold my phone to the window, taking pictures of the crooked tree, but he's right.

The person-shaped lump is gone, which makes me wonder if he was ever really there in the first place. My stomach twists as I imagine a man out there, watching us.

I look at Billy. "How did you know he was here?"

"You ever get that feeling like something's about to go wrong?"

Goose bumps rise on my arm. I nod.

Billy's eyes get a faraway look. "I always knew when my dad was gonna lose it. I got this feeling in my stomach when it was gonna get real bad. I couldn't sleep tonight, and my mom was snoring and stuff, so I came up here to see the woods better. And there he was."

He sounds a little nuts, but not any nuttier than me hiding from tornadoes or texting my dead father. In fact, we sound a lot alike.

He rubs his eyes, and I think about how awful he must feel.

"I'll get my sleeping bag," I say. "You can sleep up here tonight."

That seems to break the spell, because he finally looks away from the window and nods.

39

THE SYRUP TO MY WAFFLE

In the morning, Billy's sleeping bag is empty. I walk downstairs, stretching my stiff arms with a groan, but when I get to the kitchen, it takes me a minute to process what I'm seeing.

There are booby traps everywhere.

And I mean *everywhere*.

Loops of twine connect the kitchen chairs to the doorway, where spike balls hang from the ceiling, ready to deploy. More twine stretches across the wide entrance to the den. Billy is passed out on the couch, his arms flung over his head. His face is peaceful.

Shailene's up, though. She's sitting at the kitchen table with her head in her hands. I wonder if Billy told her about the person-shaped lump from last night, or if

it's up to me to say something. She needs to know, but I'd rather it came from him.

Stan ducks under a spike ball to hand her a cup of coffee. "Good morning," he says to me, as if it's perfectly normal that our house looks like it's been attacked by angry elves.

"Sorry about the mess," Shailene says. "That boy loves booby traps more than balloons love air." She gives a weak laugh, but her eyes are rimmed in red.

I poke my head through a gap in the twine. "It's kind of like a game, right?"

She smiles a little.

"Have a seat," Stan says. "I'll make you a waffle." He has the big waffle press out on the counter. Another Saturday tradition from me and Mom. Sometimes we mix cheese and sausage into the batter to make stuffed waffles, but Stan is a purist. He makes the batter exactly by the recipe, including sifting the flour even though Mom says sifting flour is nonsense. I watch him measure out a ladle of batter and pour it evenly over the waffle grid.

The clock reads 7:22. Mom must not be home from work yet.

I should tell them what happened, but I don't know how to start. None of the pictures on my phone show anything. There's no proof of what we saw. Cress would tell me to wait until I had evidence, but the last thing I want is Mr. Holcomb coming back here again.

A few minutes later, Stan ducks under the spike balls and drops a fresh golden waffle on my plate, along with a bottle of Grade B maple syrup. Dad used to say that Grade A syrup wasn't "the real stuff" because it's too thin and sweet. Grade B syrup is from later in the season, so it's darker and grittier, with real maple flavor.

Shailene watches me drizzle syrup over my waffle.

Then she watches me cut it into neat squares.

"You want some?" I ask, but she shakes her head.

The garage door opens and shuts, and Mom walks up to the kitchen doorway in her mint-green nurse's scrubs with Frankie on her heels and a church-shaped box of Munchkins in her hand. "Oh," she says as she takes in the traps. "Is everyone okay?"

"Getting there," Stan says. He dodges the spike balls and gives Mom a quick kiss, then whispers something in her ear. She looks from us to Billy, asleep on the couch.

"Sorry about the mess," Shailene repeats.

Stan goes back to the waffle maker while Mom steps carefully over the twine and puts her bag down, then slides her feet out of her shoes to wiggle some life into her sock-footed toes. She sets the Munchkins on the table and Frankie puts her paw on my knee, begging for food as Mom sinks into the chair next to me. Her warm hand squeezes my shoulder. Her green eyes settle on mine. Then her gaze shifts to Shailene, who's waiting, her shoulders rounded.

"How are you holding up?" Mom says.

Shailene sighs. "He's never been this bad before. I know it's not right, him acting like this, building booby traps all over creation." She wipes at her face. "We should go."

"Will running really help?" Mom says.

"I won't let him terrorize us like this," Shailene says, her eyes going hard.

Frankie gives a soft whine and I slip her a dry square of waffle.

Shailene glances at Billy. "I love him, you know. He's everything to me. He's the syrup to my waffle." Her voice isn't full of anger this time, just a whole lot of love and worry. If I tell her what we saw, it'll make her feel worse, but she deserves to know the truth.

Usually, this is where I freak out. This time, words bubble up inside of me.

"I know why he did this," I say. They look at me. I take a deep breath and remind myself that what I saw was real. "We saw someone in the woods last night."

Concern clouds Mom's eyes. "What do you mean, Mads?"

247

This is it. The moment of truth, when I have to tell her the one thing she doesn't want to hear. I have to cry wolf. "I think it was Billy's dad."

"Where?" Stan says. "What exactly did you see?"

They listen closely as I talk, and when I finish, it's quiet for a long moment. The clock ticks on the wall. While I was talking, Shailene's face was angry, but now she's scary calm.

"Enough," she says to no one in particular. She looks at me. "If I report this, will you make a statement to the police about what you saw?"

I look at Mom, who nods.

"Yes," I say. "I will."

40

ELSEWHERE

An officer comes to the house and Billy and I tell him what we saw. When we finish, Stan says it's time for a field trip, and I have never been happier for a Stan Saturday.

This time, we go downtown to one of my favorite places in Greensboro, a museum called Elsewhere. It started as a thrift shop, but now there are artists who work upstairs and open their studios for tours sometimes. There are three floors of weird stuff, including a texture library, sculptures made of baby dolls, rolls of vintage fabric, toy phones, egg cartons, suitcases, and anything else you can imagine. Dad brought me here after I hot-glued his screwdrivers into a drying rack for crab-apple slices (Frankie's favorite).

Now I'm bringing Stan here.

"Wow," he says as we walk through the front door and come face-to-face with the endless pile of stuff. The bustle of downtown Greensboro cuts off as the door shuts behind us.

Stan's eyes are wide behind his glasses, but Billy's got his arms crossed. "This stuff's all busted," he says, toeing a kiddie wagon that's missing its wheels.

"Some of it's pretty cool, though." I grab an old metal pulley off the table next to him. "It's not for sale, but you can build whatever you want while we're here."

Billy doesn't say anything, but his eyes linger on the pulley.

We pay for admission, and Billy wanders off while Stan and I dig through the bins at the front of the store. The objects are grouped by kind and color. Dad loved that this store found a new use for everything and that nothing ever went to waste. He said the idea that something disappears when we throw it away is wrong. Nothing vanishes, no matter how much we'd like to think so. Like he said, everything goes somewhere.

"What do we do?" Stan asks in an almost-whisper.

"You can play with stuff. Or look around. Or create something. It's up to you."

He nods, but his brow furrows as he follows me around the tables.

The suitcases on the top shelves are my favorite. Each one has a paper tag hanging from a thin white string. I like to imagine that they're full of all the weird stuff from people's lives. If I could only keep a suitcase worth of things, I'd take Dad's picture, and Croc, and Mom's rolling pin, but also the plans I found in the attic, and my photo albums, and the little box of things I've collected from my trips with Stan. I didn't intend to do it. The ticket stubs and pamphlets had piled up, and last week, I put them in a shoe box. Now Stan is part of my collection, too.

"We should do it," I say to Stan, and his brows rise.

"Do what?"

"The house plans from Dad. We should build the room for the baby. If that's okay."

Stan smiles. "Of course it's okay. Tell you what, how about we talk to John about it? Maybe his company can do the work."

"Can it be a surprise for Mom?"

"We can do our best." Stan beams like we're accomplices, and a warm glow gathers in my belly, like I've had a big mug of hot chocolate. On my own, there isn't much I can do to surprise Mom. But I'm not on my own anymore. And soon there will be *four* of us.

Billy appears from around the corner. "You have to see what's upstairs."

Stan hangs back, letting us run up on our own.

At the top of the stairs is a giant mobile—a sculpture made of all kinds of stuff, like a ladle tied to a garden rake that's hanging from a pair of pantyhose, which is also connected to an old bike tire. Billy tips the end of the ladle, and the whole thing moves, dipping and rotating.

"That's so cool," I say, and he nods.

"Are you excited about your new place?" I ask.

He shrugs. "I don't know."

"Do you like your room?"

"It's kind of cool," he says with a tiny smile. "There's a closet with a secret passage."

"No *way*."

He grins, and the room gets quiet. It's just us and the mobile, slowly twisting through the air. It's weird to think Billy and Shailene will be moving out soon, now that I've gotten used to them being there.

On our way out, I see a pile of action figures, and mixed among the soldiers and cowboys is an astronaut. He's a perfect fit for the *Friendship 7*, with his big white back-pack and his shiny metal visor. I wonder if the museum would make an exception to their rules in the name of saving a "friendship." I take a picture of the astronaut and text it to Cress.

41

THE LAST DAY

There are days that feel like endings, like the last day of summer vacation or the last day of school. On days like those, something is over but something new is about to begin. It's sad but good, in a way. That's how it feels in our house on Sunday.

We all know that on Monday morning, Billy and his mom are leaving.

It's also the last full day I have to work on my Living Museum project. Our presentations are on Wednesday. My costume's ready, but I still need to finish Miss Rivera's packet. Most of the questions are basic—your person's name, where they were born, what they accomplished—but there is one question that I'm stuck on:

If this person could give you one piece of advice, what would it be?

I can remember a lot of things Dad used to say, but I don't know what he'd say to *me*.

Standing in my room, wearing clothes that look like Dad's, with his plans and surveyor stand in front of me, I don't know which step to take next. It feels like Dad is the most gone he's ever been. Like every trace of him has floated away, out the window and into the woods.

My chest is tight as I text him. "Are you there, Dad?"

I spend way too long staring at my phone, waiting for a reply that will never come.

Cooking sounds travel up through the floorboards. Mom and Shailene have decided that a special Sunday dinner is in order for Billy and his mom's last night here, which is another one of those weird ending-and-beginning moments. I think of the day that everyone we knew came to our house after Dad died. No one wore black because he wouldn't have wanted it that way. I remember how Mom said we would have a party to say good-bye, and how sometimes it felt like a party, but other times it felt the way I do now, so heavy I can't lift my foot to take a single step.

There's a knock at my door.

I expect Billy to pop in—he's out in the garage with Frankie—but it's Mom who appears. Her mouth opens when she sees me, standing there looking like a sad imitation of Dad.

I start to cry, and she's at my side, her arms around me.

She holds me while I make all those awful noises that go along with breaking your heart.

"Oh, my girl," she says, pressing me to her. "Look at you." Her fingers trail Dad's plaid shirt, which I've rolled up to fit my arms. Her eyes get shiny. I know how this must look.

"It's for the Living Museum at school," I say. "Everyone dresses up as someone important from history. I'm going as Dad." I have everything on that I'm taking to school. Everything but the mustache, which I'm planning to draw on with Mom's eyeliner pencil.

"Oh," Mom says. Her eyes travel to the surveyor's stand. *"Oh."*

"I need to know what advice he would give me. For my project," I say, trying not to hiccup. "I found everything else, but I don't know what he would say."

Mom nods slowly, then leads us to my bed, where we sit with Croc in my lap. His purple plush has worn through in places, revealing the webbing underneath.

"I wish I'd known what you were working on,"

255

Mom says. "You shouldn't have to do this alone, honey. I'm sorry I've been so distracted with Shailene and the baby—"

"It's okay."

"No, it's not," she says, "but I'm here now. What is it you need to know?"

I show her the packet, and she reads the question:

If this person could give you one piece of advice, what would it be?

"Well," she says. "I think your dad would say it's not your job to save everyone else. Sometimes you have to let other people take care of you, too."

"But he died because of me."

"No, honey," Mom says. She takes my hands in hers. "What happened to your father was an accident. It was a terrible, horrible accident that no one could have seen coming, but it's not your fault. He made a choice, Maddy. He chose you."

I hear what she's saying, but I still feel guilty.

"If I could change it, I would," she says softly. "I would give anything to bring him back." She takes a breath and looks me in the eyes. "I love your father so much, bug. I miss him, too. I'll always miss him. Just because someone's gone doesn't mean you stop loving them, even if you start loving someone else. There's room in your heart to love so many people. I think Dad would want us to be a family again. He'd want that for us."

She smiles, and I know she's right. Maybe I don't have to choose between Dad and Stan. Maybe I can keep them both. A weight lifts off my heart.

"I think it's wonderful that you're going to share your father's story with your friends," Mom says. "He will never be forgotten. Not for one moment. Not ever."

The pressure in my chest fades. It's not going away forever, but for now I can breathe.

"Do you want to do the safety checks?" Mom asks in her gentlest voice.

I start to say yes, but then I realize that what I want more than a familiar routine is to show Mom everything I've gathered about Dad. To share it with her and to hear her stories about him, which say so much more than any fact can ever tell.

"Can you tell me about the night you met at the fair?" I ask.

"Of course," she says. "It was one of the best nights of my life."

42

GOOD-BYE

With Billy and Shailene there, the kitchen is full, but we've learned how to work together. Even Frankie knows that Billy is her best bet for treats now. She never strays far from his side, even when I drop an accidental potato peel on the floor. By the evening, there's enough food for an army, and it smells like a holiday has arrived.

Only this is no holiday—it's good-bye.

When everything's ready, we tear into the food: quiche lorraine, cucumber salad, roasted pork shoulder, mashed potatoes, and spoon bread. There are pies for dessert, too, but they're cooling in the kitchen. Billy eats everything, but he's back to being quiet.

I flick a kernel of corn at him, and he scowls. A few minutes later, he pokes me with his elbow and says, "Try to say S-N-I-K-E without sounding Australian."

"Snike," I say, and we giggle at the sound of it.

"Snike."

"Snike!"

Like any Sunday dinner, there's way too much food. Stan leans back in his chair, patting his lean belly like it's invisibly expanded. Mom and Shailene spend most of the meal talking to each other. We're clearing the table when my phone pings. It's a text from Cress. She loves the picture of the little astronaut I sent her from Elsewhere, which she agrees is the perfect touch for her *Friendship 7* model. She's going to use the idea.

"YAY!" I text back. Then I add, "I would never squish your model."

After a pause, another text bubble appears. I hold my breath, waiting to see what Cress will say. Finally, the words pop up.

"I know. ☺ So are you going to tell me what's up?"

I can imagine Cress at her house, probably sitting on her neatly made bed with a book propped on her knees. Or a word puzzle. Or maybe her family is having one of their epic Scrabble matches. I'm not supposed to tell

Cress that Billy and Shailene are living here, but they're moving out tomorrow. I'm tired of keeping secrets from my best friend.

While everyone's chatting and cleaning up, I text Cress the whole story about Billy and Shailene. How I kept looking for more information, especially after Cress agreed that Eric looked an awful lot like Billy Holcomb. How Miss Rivera gave me a list of online newspapers to research over Easter, and how I found a picture of Billy Holcomb's dad that matched Eric's sweatshirt. How Billy's dad showed up at the pig pickin' and set all the secrets into motion.

I text for so long that my fingers get tired and autocorrect has to save me from spouting pure garbage. It's a lot to write, and my heart pounds as I think of Cress reading the whole story.

"Let's put the pies on the table," I say to Billy.

"What kind of pies?"

"Toll House," I say. "And lemon."

He grins.

We carry the pies to the table and straighten the place mats and silverware. No one has room for pie right now, but they'll be here waiting for us, whenever we're ready.

We go back into the kitchen and find the grown-ups in tears, only this time it's from laughter. "Frankie might need to go out," Stan says, cough-laughing, his cheeks pink.

"I took her out before we ate."

"Well, she may have had a little too much pork," Mom says.

Billy makes a face all of a sudden. "SBD alert!" he says, wrinkling up his nose and coughing. That's when the smell hits me: raw cabbage at full volume.

"Oh my gosh, Frankie!"

Frankie pops up at the sound of her name, tail wagging like what she's done is a good thing. I wrap my arm around her. God knows I love Frankie, but her farts are the actual worst.

My phone rings. It's Cress.

"Mads! Are you for real? Eric is the kid that went missing and he's *living at your house?*"

"I know," I say, trying to catch my breath from laughing so hard my sides hurt.

I start telling Cress about what happened.

With the phone pressed against my ear, I don't hear the door to the garage open and shut. It's not until Frankie growls that I look up and see Billy's father standing in the doorway.

43

LOST

The second I see him, I know we're lost. Mr. Holcomb's face is made of rage. His eyes are red, his mouth twisted. Gone are the sunglasses and the sweatshirt, but his tan skin and salt-and-pepper hair are the same as in the picture I found. His right arm is cocked behind his back in an odd way. "Hello, son," he says, in this very quiet voice.

Next to me, Billy goes completely still.

Shailene half screams, and I lurch back, bumping Billy into the wall. The door to the living room is behind me, and beyond that, Dad's field, and escape. I've spent so much time preparing for the worst, and now here it is. The Biggest Bad I have ever faced.

But I'm frozen.

I clutch Frankie to my side. She growls and growls while Mom slowly turns to face the doorway. Stan is next to her, his hand on her shoulder.

"Everyone stay calm," Mom says in her nurse's voice.

Billy's father ignores her. His eyes shift to Shailene. "You think you can take him away from me? Well, you're wrong." He takes a step toward Billy.

"Whoa," Stan says, getting in front of us. "Can I help you, buddy?"

"This is none of your business," Mr. Holcomb growls.

"That may be true, but this is my house."

Mr. Holcomb smiles. It's a slow and slippery thing that makes my stomach turn. He whips a handgun from behind his back and points it at Stan's face.

Shailene makes a strangled sort of sound.

Cress's voice crackles in my ear. "What's going on? Is something wrong?"

I don't dare answer her.

"Why don't we all sit down and talk this out," Mom says, holding her hands up like she means no harm, but Billy's dad is having none of it.

"Give me what's mine, and I'll go."

Billy's breath comes quick and shallow from behind me.

"That's not going to happen," Stan says.

Mr. Holcomb thumbs the hammer.

"No!" Shailene shouts.

Cress is still in my ear, asking questions. She knows something's wrong, but I can't answer. There's no way I can manage to hang up and dial 911 without him noticing, either.

My eyes dart around the kitchen, searching for a solution. The knife by the cutting board. The phone. *The emergency button.* When I see it, a sound escapes me.

Mr. Holcomb's eyes cut my way. He puts his hand out. "Give me the phone."

Mom's eyes meet mine. *Do what he says,* they say.

I know I should, but I'm not ready yet.

I thought if I anticipated every little thing that might go wrong, I could save us, but that's impossible. Things will always go wrong. All we can do is make our choices.

Stan reaches for me. He wants me to give him the phone, and then he'll hand it to Billy's dad. This is my chance. The emergency button isn't that far away. Maybe five steps. It'll take a while for the police to come, but if I hand the phone to Stan, it might distract Billy's dad long enough that I can make it there without him noticing.

Billy steps out from behind Stan. "I'm not scared of you," he says to his father, and I take the opportunity to step toward the button.

Mr. Holcomb laughs. "You would be if you had a lick

of sense, but we both know that's not the case, now, don't we." His eyes cut back to me. "The phone. *Now*."

I let my weight pour into my right foot, keeping one hand on Frankie's collar. She growls and pulls, but if I let her go, she could get hurt. I'll have to drag her with me.

I reach to give the phone to Stan and lean toward the emergency button.

Cress's voice gets tiny and far away.

For the first time in forever, I don't feel like I'm tipping over the edge of something. The floor is solid beneath my feet. The phone touches Stan's open palm. He grabs it. Mr. Holcomb's eyes follow the phone, and I dodge sideways, toward the emergency button.

"Stay where you are!" he shouts.

My finger reaches the button.

He cocks the gun.

The button clicks.

Mr. Holcomb's eyes bulge, the gun wavering. For a moment, it seems like there's a chance we will get out of this okay. Somehow he won't understand what I've done and the police will get here in time and he'll be captured and we'll all be fine.

I believe that might really happen, too—until the house phone rings.

That's what happens when you press the alarm. The

company gets the signal, and then they call to see if you're okay. If we are, we have to give them our password to prove it.

Only this time everything is not okay.

The phone rings again, and Billy's father stumbles back.

The gun jerks in my direction.

Mom screams.

Stan leaps in front of me.

The gun goes off.

44

The day my father died, we went to the beach to dig for mole crabs. Some people call them sand fleas, but we call them diggers. When a wave crashes into the beach, the water spreads over the sand like a fan unfolding before it turns back and runs into the sea. The stretch of wet sand left behind is where the diggers live. They pop up as the waves rush over the beach and burrow back into the sand as the water recedes.

Mole crabs are my favorite to catch. Their little legs scratch like sandpaper against my skin, but they don't bite—they just want to get back to the sand.

That day, we went down to the beach with a little plastic rake and a bucket to keep the diggers for a little while, but not too long or they would overheat in the morning sun. Mom lagged behind at the rental house, packing a lunch for later. She said she'd meet us out there.

The tide was still high, and the water had carved a kind of shelf into the dry sand of the beach, creating a drop-off, like a tall ledge that ran along the edge of the water.

We could hear the waves crashing into it.

Crash, crash, crash.

"We'll walk farther up," Dad said, taking my hand.

I went to swing, but without Mom there I flopped against his legs, so he lifted me up onto his shoulders even though I was too big for that. We walked along the edge of the sand cliff, headed for the smooth stretch of beach up ahead where the diggers would be plentiful. I loved that first dip into the water. The ocean is always much colder than you expect, and alive. Frothy with bubbles and sand and bits of seaweed and shells. I always screamed when my toes hit the water, but it was a thrill to run down and back, chasing the waves and daring them to catch me.

I was falling before I knew what happened.

It was like the drop on a roller coaster—a sudden weightlessness, the sky spinning before me, flashing water then sky then water again.

The sand shelf had given way beneath us like an

44

JUNE 2

iceberg breaking off a glacier, only the sand sank, leaving nothing to hold on to. No life raft.

Just me and Dad, tossed into the ocean where the riptide waited, hidden beneath the blue-gray surface of the water. We plunged beneath the waves, white water crashing over our heads. I knew how to swim, but not in that water, deep and cold and tossing all around. Dad's hands clasped my waist and lifted me up. I broke the surface and gasped for air.

"It's okay," he shouted. "I'm here."

There was blood on his forehead, but he was strong enough to hold me up while he swam along the shelf of sand, looking for a way up and out of that water. The tide fought him, pulling us down with every wave. He called out, his arms shaking. We spun beneath a wave, but he didn't let go. It seemed impossible, that we couldn't claw our way up that shelf of sand and out of there, but the ocean is a million times stronger than a single human being.

A surging wave lifted us up again, and Mom's head appeared at the edge of the sand shelf. Her arms reached for me. Dad lifted me up, and Mom snatched hold of my fingers so hard that I screamed, but she didn't let go, not until she had me clear of the water.

As soon as I hit dry sand, she leaned back over the

edge, reaching for Dad, but he had slipped below the waves. We waited and waited, but he didn't come back up.

That is how I lived.

And that is how he died.

45

MAN DOWN

For a moment after the gun goes off, everyone freezes, including Billy's dad. Openmouthed horror spreads over his face, as if he's been possessed by a devil that has only just let go. He stares at the gun, then drops it to the floor, his hand shaking. He steps back, and Frankie somehow manages to slip out of my grasp. She charges at him, and he runs. Out of the kitchen, out of the house, with Frankie tearing after him, barking her head off.

Relief pours through my veins.

Then I see the blood.

"Honey!" Mom cries, reaching for Stan as he slides to the floor.

Stan's face is even paler than usual, his cheeks two red spots on a background of paper white.

Mom's hands run over him, searching. "Where is it? Honey, where did it hit?"

Stan lifts a trembling hand toward his thigh, and my stomach lurches when I see the blood pouring from his leg like a geyser. A lake of red spreads across the kitchen tiles.

Mom presses down on the wound. "Quick, Mads. The dish towel!"

I snatch the towel from the oven bar and hand it to Mom. She rips it down the middle but not all the way, making it twice as long, and fastens it around Stan's leg.

"You're fine," she says. "You're going to be fine."

I want to believe her, but I feel like I'm sinking beneath the waves again. It's hard to imagine there's any blood left in Stan's body.

Shailene joins Mom on the floor and presses her hands to Stan's leg.

Time seems to stop.

I'm frozen again.

Long minutes pass with Mom talking urgently to Shailene and on the phone.

Someone shouts outside. Then a chorus of voices. Yelling, demanding. I start toward the front door to see what's happening, but Mom says, "No, Maddy! Stay here!"

Then I hear Frankie barking, and my heart leaps into my throat.

I run to the front door as Mom shouts for me to come back, but I can already see red and blue lights flashing outside.

"The police are here!" I shout.

Billy comes running.

There's an officer halfway between the house and the court, in the woods. He's kneeling over Mr. Holcomb, who is facedown on the ground as Frankie circles, barking. One of Billy's spike balls swings lazily overhead, winding down from having been triggered.

"Got him," Billy says.

In the kitchen, Stan cries out, and I know what I have to do.

I throw the door open. "Help! We need help!"

The officer finishes securing Mr. Holcomb's handcuffs and comes running. Behind him, another police car pulls into our driveway. The man who steps out is broad, with a tall hat.

Sheriff Dobbs.

The officer reaches me. It's the same man who came to the house before.

"It's my stepdad," I say. "He's been shot."

"Ten forty-three, man down," the officer calls into his radio as he jogs down the hall to the kitchen. I can hear Mom's voice, urgent. My knees turn to rubber as I think of Stan lying there, of the blood on the tiles, and all I know is that I don't want to lose him, too.

46

A NEW PUZZLE

The last time I rode in an ambulance, it was without my father. He was in his own ambulance, ahead of us. What I didn't know was that he was already dead.

This time, I'm in a separate ambulance behind Mom and Stan's. Billy and his mom are with me. Billy's gripping my fingers like his life depends on it.

When we get to the hospital, Stan's stretcher rushes ahead, and Mom runs over to wrap me in her arms. She's trying not to cry, but her body gives her away with big, jerking breaths. She pulls back and looks at me, right in the eyes, and says, "I'm here. I'm right here, Maddy."

I know she is, but a part of me is floating above us now, apart from everything.

It's like the barrier has reappeared, only now it cuts me off from the entire world.

We sit in the waiting area while Stan is in surgery. The bullet hit an artery in his leg and they have to repair it. After a while, Sheriff Dobbs appears. He says something to me, but I don't hear him the first time. He takes off his hat and sits down next to me.

"Your friend called us," he says. "She wouldn't get off the phone until we promised to go to your house. We got the safety alert, too, and, well, you did good, kid."

I think of Cress and my eyes flood with tears again.

Eventually, Sheriff Dobbs goes away. Other people come and go.

Cress and her family show up, with Mia, too. We hug, and Cress gives me a bracelet she's made for me out of little white beads that spell my name. A simple thing, but pretty, with sparkly beads on either end.

I slip the bracelet over my arm and we sit back down together.

While we wait, the police give us our space, but they hover by the door.

I think back to all those times I wished that Dad were there instead of Stan, and my heart sinks a little lower.

More than anything, I want Stan to be okay. To go on goofy field trips together. To talk about computers and build new rooms for our house. But all I can do is wait.

After what feels like a century, Stan is out of surgery and we go back to see him. My throat closes as Mom opens the door, but once we're inside the recovery room, we find Stan propped at a gentle angle in a hospital bed with his little red notebook in his hand.

"Oh, honey," Mom says, collapsing against his shoulder. She clutches him, and Stan clutches her back. After a minute, he pulls away enough to give me a little wave like he isn't sure if I'm glad to see him, and the rest of that barrier falls away, shattered into pieces.

I run to the bed and hug him. He hugs me back.

"It's okay," he says. "I'm okay."

"No you're not. You got shot." A hiccup of tears escapes me.

"The bullet missed the bone," he says in his matter-of-fact way. "And they say there isn't much muscle damage. Just bad luck with the artery, that's all. I should be good to go in no time."

I can't help smiling. Encyclopedia Stan. Spouting facts and writing in his little red notebook like always.

I pull back and pick up the notebook, waving it in front of him.

"Really? You're taking notes now? What's in this thing, anyway?"

He hesitates. Looks at Mom. She nods.

"Well, actually. Quite a lot about you."

"What?"

"Go on. Open it," Mom says with a smile.

I do, and inside I find a journal that starts on the day of the Greek Festival. The day Stan and I first met. Every entry is about the things we've done together, the times our field trips fell flat—like the ropes course—and the times we clicked, like the night at the observatory. There are also notes on things I like (vanilla ice cream, churros, corn dogs, painting with my fingers, and collecting leaves and acorns) and things I don't like (heights, chocolate ice cream, rainbow sprinkles, getting lost, and sitting still for too long).

I can't believe Stan kept track of all of this.

I can't believe he *noticed*.

His cheeks are pink with embarrassment. He clears his throat, picking at the edge of his hospital blanket. "I haven't been a dad before," he says. "I wanted to get it right."

That's when the puzzle rearranges, and I see that it's

not the same puzzle at all. Not anymore. It's a new puzzle, and in this one, Stan fits perfectly. With one simple turn, he drops right into place. It's not fair that Dad is gone, but there is this new life right in front of me.

"I'm sorry about what I said," I blurt. "About you not being my real dad."

"I know," Stan says. "From what I've read, that's a perfectly normal reaction to this kind of life change, but I'm glad we're friends now."

"Not friends," I say. "Family."

He smiles. "I like the sound of that."

47

NEXT

It's weird to go back to the regular world after something huge has happened, but that is what we do. It's the only thing you can do, really. Billy isn't living with us anymore. Mr. Jessup helped him and his mom move into their new place over the last few days.

Their whole future is ahead of them.

As I get ready for the Living Museum, Stan is still in the hospital. He's going to get discharged anytime now. His leg is healing well, but the doctors want to be sure. You can't be too careful with an arterial graft, according to Stan. After two days in the hospital, he's become an expert on the anatomy of the human thigh.

I finish putting on my outfit: Dad's old flannel, dirty jeans (his were always dirty), brown work boots, his hard hat and reflective vest. The surveyor's stand is folded up in my book bag, and the models I've made of his level and compass are waiting in the art room at school. I use Mom's brown eyeliner to draw on a big goofy mustache, using Dad's photo as a guide.

I laugh, thinking of how happy Mom was when he shaved it off—but suddenly I can't remember what he looked like without the mustache in my photo.

This empty feeling hits my stomach. It feels like Dad's leaving me, or that maybe he's already gone. I grab my phone, fingers fumbling, and text him.

"I got your stuff from the attic, and I'm supposed to act like you, but I don't know if I can do it. I don't know if you can hear me, but I—"

My phone hiccups. It does this sometimes, when I use voice-to-text.

After a second, the screen unfreezes and the words fill in on their own.

"—I love you."

Most people would probably say it's a fluke, but that's not what this is.

This is a message from Dad.

I read the text over and over. Then I sling my book bag over my shoulder and head downstairs so Mom can take me to school.

It's strange walking into the gym dressed as Dad, but everyone else is dressed up, too. There are kids in white beards, kids in suits and sparkly leotards. There's even an astronaut with a big white helmet on, and every other kind of outfit you can imagine.

Everyone has a red plastic cup. We're supposed to hold the cup out and the grown-ups give us their spare change to hear a story about the person we're dressed up as.

It's a museum, but alive. A *living* museum.

The gym vibrates with voices and laughter. Everywhere you look, people are smiling.

As I cross the springy wood floor looking for the rest of my class, Miss Rivera hurries up to me. She's dressed very differently—in a satiny two-piece suit with lace trim and a feathered cap. Her shiny black hair is tied back in a bun beneath the cap. She makes a quick bow.

"Greetings, fair student," she says. "From what era do you hail?"

"The twenty-first century."

"Excellent. I am from the 1660s, when women were first allowed to take the stage in England. Did you know that until then, it was illegal for women to perform?"

"No."

"Now you do." She smiles and rests a hand on my shoulder. "All set for today?" There's concern in her eyes, but for once it doesn't feel like a judgment. More like love.

"I think so. I have my speech." I hold up my notecards.

She gives me a thumbs-up and starts to leave, then spins back around and says, more quietly amid the din of the gymnasium, so that only I can hear, "Thank you, Maddy."

"For what?"

"I'm auditioning for the Greensboro Players Theatre next week. Wish me luck!"

She hurries off and I turn to find myself face-to-face with the astronaut I saw earlier. Cress is next to him in her Katherine Johnson costume. He lifts his visor. Diesel's face appears.

"I'm her astronaut," he says. "John Glenn."

Cress smiles, her braces gleaming. "I saved his life."

Diesel blushes red.

"Where's Billy?" I ask. "Didn't he come with you?"

Cress points. "He's over there."

I turn to look. Billy is there, looking about as comfortable as a crab in a crab trap, standing with Cress's parents and Mr. Jessup and Shailene, who is fussing with Billy's black bow tie. I can't tell who he is, exactly. Is that an old telephone?

He sees me and waves. Then he walks over to us.

He's wearing a dress jacket and the black bow tie and shiny black shoes, but what's interesting is that there's an old phone cord wrapped all around him.

"Who are you?" I ask.

He gives me that half grin of his. "Alexander Graham Bell. He invented the telephone. I think I might like to invent stuff, too." He stares at my face. "Nice mustache."

My cheeks go hot. "Thanks."

He looks at me, and I get that buzzing feeling in my chest again.

"I miss Frankie," he says.

"Even her SBDs?"

He laughs. "No, not those."

"How's your new place?"

"It's good," he says with another big smile. "Mom said we can get a dog soon."

He and Diesel start arguing about what kind of dog he should get, and as we all stand there talking, I see Mom on her way into the gym. She's pushing a wheelchair—and Stan is in it! His pale face is flushed, but in a good way. My family.

I wave, and they wave back.

For a split second, everything tilts, and I can feel the future rushing at us. I don't know what's next, but whatever it is, good or bad, I know we'll face it together.

ACKNOWLEDGMENTS

As a child, I often wondered what it would be like to find a missing person. The idea both excited and terrified me. What would happen if I saw a child from one of those missing persons notices? Would I be able to help? Would anyone listen to me? Those are the questions that led me to Maddy's story, and I am eternally grateful to everyone who helped me tell it.

First, thank you to everyone who works in support of domestic abuse survivors. I spoke with many advocates in various fields, and their generous insights are what allowed me to portray these families with any degree of authenticity or accuracy. Any faults that persist are mine and mine alone.

Thank you to Marisa White, vice principal of North Johnston Middle School of Johnston County, North Carolina; Camilla Hicks, North Carolina licensed social worker; Jeana Lungwitz, JD, clinical professor and supporting attorney for the Domestic Violence Clinic at the University of Texas School of Law (and Daniel Graver for connecting us); Yolanda Smith, licensed paralegal in North Carolina (and Kim Freund Graver, Meredith Kincaid, and Nora Sullivan for connecting us); Dr. Laurie B. Levine, PhD, marriage and family therapist and former Domestic Violence Agency clinical director; Ingrid L. Eubanks, North Carolina licensed attorney; and the clerks at the Guilford County, North Carolina, General Court of Justice, District Court Division.

This story took on many forms before it found the right one, and I'm so grateful to Tracey Keevan for always believing in these characters and in what I had to say. It's rare that someone else understands what I'm trying to do and tells me to go for it. That faith and patience allowed me to find the very best version of this story and make it shine. Thank you also to Esther Cajahuaringa, Christine Collins, Phil Buchanan, Christine Saunders, Dina Sherman, and the entire Disney Hyperion team.

To my agent, Elena Giovinazzo: Your unwavering faith and support means everything. I love being a part of the Pippin team! Thank you also to Holly McGhee, Larissa Helena, Ashley Valentine, and everyone at Pippin Properties, Inc.

Writing is a team sport, and I am grateful to have many wonderful and supportive friends. Thank you to Jenn Bishop for an insightful early read, Lindsay Eager for helping me decipher my own words, Peter Knapp for supporting this book when it was still five stories stuck together, Laura Shovan for steadfast friendship, Leatrice McKinney and her grandmother for the "I love you" texts, Lois Sepahban for the hugs, Rebecca Sutton for the cheers, Heidi Heilig, Leah Henderson, Colten Hibbs, Sarah Lemon, Hay Farris, the #mgbetareaders, Fight Me, Words Bookstore in Maplewood, New Jersey, the South Orange Public Library and Keisha Miller, and my Novel Bites: Michelle, Barbara, Christine (and Imy!), Bridget, Melissa, Romaine, and Léana.

To my sister: Thank you for everything. You are the kindest, most helpful person I know and I'm lucky that you're stuck with me for life.

To my parents: You have always believed in me, so I have always believed, too. Thank you for that gift, and for giving it to my children as well.

To Andrew: You didn't want to be thanked, so of course I'm thanking you! Thank you for getting me through the ugly parts with love and patience.

To Perry and Alec: Thank you for the creative swears, and for being as excited about this book as I am. It's your book, too.

To Charlotte: Thank you for the kisses.

This book was brought to you by my favorite tracks played on repeat, including: "Cosmic Love" by Florence and the Machine, "Running Up That Hill" by Meg Myers, "Midnight City" by M83, "Die Young" by Sylvan Esso, "Got You (Where I Want You)" by the Flys, everything Chvrches, "La marcheuse" by Christine and the Queens, and "Bike Dream" by Rostam, among others.

For anyone in the United States who is experiencing domestic violence, seeking resources or information, or questioning unhealthy aspects of their relationship, the National Domestic Violence Hotline is available 24/7 at 1-800-799-7233 or TTY 1-800-787-3224.